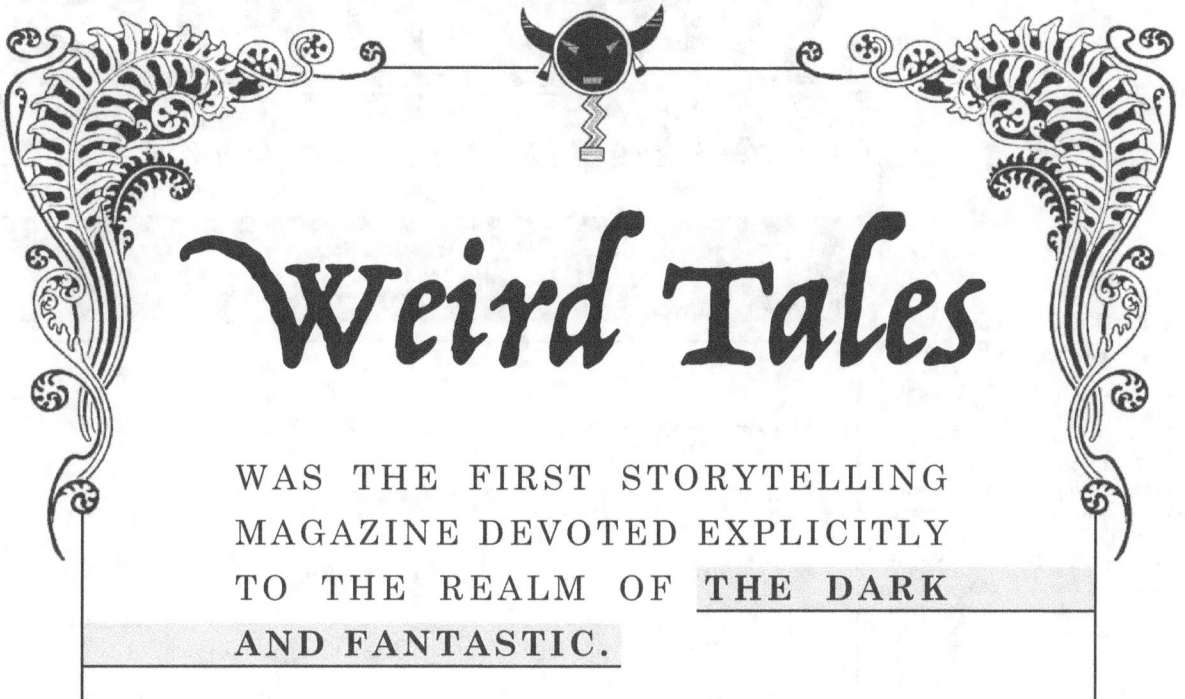

Weird Tales

WAS THE FIRST STORYTELLING MAGAZINE DEVOTED EXPLICITLY TO THE REALM OF **THE DARK AND FANTASTIC.**

ORIGINALLY LAUNCHED BACK IN 1923, *WEIRD TALES* PROVIDED A LITERARY HOME FOR SUCH DIVERSE WIELDERS OF THE IMAGINATION AS **H.P. LOVECRAFT** (CREATOR OF CTHULHU), **ROBERT E. HOWARD** (CREATOR OF CONAN THE BARBARIAN), **MARGARET BRUNDAGE** (ARTISTIC GODMOTHER OF GOTH FETISHISM), AND **RAY BRADBURY** (AUTHOR OF *SOMETHING WICKED THIS WAY COMES* AND *FAHRENHEIT 451*).

TODAY, O WONDROUS READER OF THE 21ST CENTURY, WE CONTINUE TO SEEK OUT THAT WHICH IS MOST WEIRD AND UNSETTLING, FOR YOUR OWN EDIFICATION AND ALARM.

PUBLISHER John Gregory Betancourt
EDITORIAL & CREATIVE DIRECTOR Stephen H. Segal FICTION EDITOR Ann VanderMeer
CONTRIBUTING EDITORS Scott Connors, Elizabeth Genco, Darrell Schweitzer
EDITOR EMERITUS George H. Scithers EDITORIAL ASSISTANT Tessa Kum
CONTRIBUTING ARTISTS Sam Heimer, Will Koffman, Ira Marcks,
Marc Robinson, Nigel Sade, Saara Salmi, Daniele Serra, Star St. Germain
ASSISTANT TO THE PUBLISHER Renee Farrah

Weird Tales

SUBSCRIBE AT WWW.WEIRDTALESMAGAZINE.COM

January–February 2008

A WILDSIDE PRESS MAGAZINE

WEIRD TALES ® is published 6 times a year by Wildside Press, LLC in association with Terminus Publishing Co., Inc. Postmaster and others: send all changes of address and other subscription matters to Wildside Press, 9710 Traville Gateway Dr. #234, Rockville MD 20850–7408. Single copies, $6.99 in U.S.A. & possessions; $7.99 by mail to Canada, $10 by first class mail elsewhere. Subscriptions: 6 issues $24 in U.S.A. & possessions; $45 elsewhere, in U.S. funds. Single-copy orders should be addressed to WEIRD TALES at the address above. Copyright © 2007 by Wildside Press, LLC. All rights reserved; reproduction prohibited without prior permission. Typeset & printed in the United States of America. WEIRD TALES ® is a registered trademark owned by Weird Tales, Limited.

Cold Tonnage Books, 22 Kings Lane, Windlesham, Surrey, GU20 6JQ, U.K., andy@coldtonnage.co.uk, offers subscriptions to WEIRD TALES at £27 for six issues in the U.K., £30 elsewhere, payment in sterling by cheques, money orders, or PayPal.

LETTERS TO THE EDITOR

Letters to the editor may be emailed to letters@weirdtales.net or snail-mailed to Weird Tales, 9710 Traville Gateway Dr. #234, Rockville MD 20850-7408. Letters may be edited for length and style.

BOOK REVIEWS, ETC.

Genre fiction books submitted for review should be sent to contributing editor Scott Connors, 4277 Larson Street Apt. 52, Marysville, CA 95901. Nonfiction, comics, weird art and music, etc., should be sent to Weird Tales, Attn: Reviews, 9710 Traville Gateway Dr. #234, Rockville MD 20850-7408.

FICTION

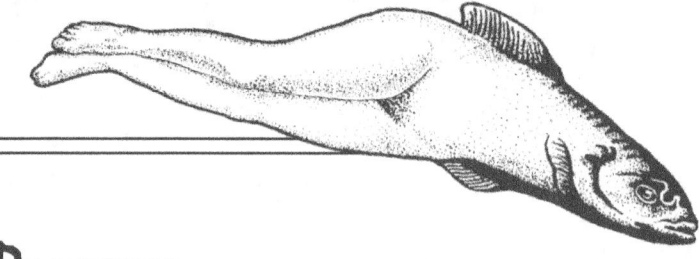

POETRY

COVER ILLUSTRATION

The Unique Magazine

"ALL WRITERS OF SUCH STORIES ARE PROPHETS"

Issue 348 ~ Vol. 63, No. 1

Features

"We have made a commitment to beat lunacy together."

Columns & Departments

MANUSCRIPT SUBMISSIONS

We read unsolicited manuscripts that are submitted in standard manuscript format. We *prefer* email submissions, addressed to **weirdtales@ gmail.com**. We also accept paper submissions addressed to **Weird Tales, P.O. Box 38190, Tallahassee FL 32315.** Paper submissions must include a return envelope, addressed to you, with enough U.S. Postage affixed to bring the manuscript back to you. If you want us to discard the manuscript if we don't buy it, simply include a business-sized envelope, addressed to you, with U.S. Postage affixed, so we can send comments.

Before submitting your manuscript, please peruse our guidelines, which are available via our Web site: **www.weirdtalesmagazine.com**. If you require a paper copy of the guidelines, send a self-addressed stamped envelope to: Wildside Press Magazines, 9710 Traville Gateway Drive #234, Rockville MD 20850-7408. (This is also the address for all subscription and business matters.)

We recommend three books on writing: *On Writing Science Fiction: the Editors Strike Back!* by Scithers, Schweitzer, & John M. Ford; $19.50, postpaid, in hardcover from Owlswick Press, P.O. Box 4001, Rockville MD 20850-7408. (Written by *Weird Tales* contributing editors.) In Maryland, add $1.19 sales tax. Another: *The Craft of Writing*, by William Sloane, available from second-hand bookstores. The third, always essential, and most important: *The Elements of Style*, by William Strunk, Jr., & E.B. White, available from any good bookstore.

We are not responsible for manuscripts in our hands or in transit.

ARE YOU MOVING?

Don't miss an issue! Send change-of-address information to us at **subs@ wildsidepress.com** or Weird Tales, 9710 Traville Gateway Dr. #234, Rockville MD 20850-7408.

The eyrie

A VIEW FROM   UNEARTHLY HEIGHTS

WEIRD TALES FANS — a couple dozen of them, at leat — had the opportunity to enjoy a bit of Hollywood glamour up close and personal in November, when we held a reading from recent WT issues at Eljay's, a bookstore on the South Side of Pittsburgh, Pennsylvania. Our surprise guest reader was none other than David Conrad, co-star of CBS's popular supernatural drama *The Ghost Whisperer*. David, though best known for his television and film roles, is a fine writer himself as well as a fine stage actor; we first met him some years ago when he performed a selection of World War I battlefield poetry at Pittsburgh's historic Carnegie Library, and his subsequent turns onstage in *Richard II* and *Henry V* garnered rave reviews from theatre critics. He brought a similarly high-caliber performance to his readings of Clayton Kroh's "The Yankee at the Sitting-Up" (issue #347) and Scott William Carter's "Directions to Mourning's Deep" (#344), and the audience was most appreciative. Many thanks to David, as well as to our two other fantastic readers: Christiane D. of the weird musical ensemble Soma Mestizo, and Robert Isenberg of the Pittsburgh Monologue Project.

Speaking of *The Ghost Whisperer* and therefore of unearthly television programs in general, it's interesting to note that, while we readerly people are accustomed to dismissing "standard TV fare" as the *opposite* of great imaginative fiction, in fact, some of the small screen's greatest moments ever have come from the briliant telling of weird tales. Most obviously and influentially, of course, is *The Twilight Zone*, which in 1959 took up WEIRD TALES's cultural sceptre as the foremost purveyor of that particular brand of strangeness lying on the shadowy boundaries between magic, science and horror. Writer-producer Rod Serling has been honored as one of the medium's finest creators ever — quite simply, because he brought true weird to the people.

In the '80s, we had David Lynch's *Twin Peaks* mining the surreal visions that lurk beneath small-town America. In the '90s, we had *The X-Files* breathing new life into the pursuit of explained Fortean phenomena. And in the '00s, we have *Lost* proving that Jules Verne didn't explore *all* the strangeness that might be found on a mysterious island. While these three shows may not match *The Twilight Zone* for sheer consistency of storytelling genius, each was a watershed television artifact of its decade, spawning not only frequent cultural references and devoted fandoms, but inferior imitators aplenty — always the most certain indicator of success in Hollywood.

Brilliant television: weird by any definition.

Online Exclusives at
WEIRDTALESMAGAZINE.COM

Throughout 2008, our Web site will be presenting a series of original essays by WEIRD TALES's newest contributing writers. We kick things off with this issue's Calvin Mills ("The Stone and Bone Boy") musing upon the essential nature of weirdness in literature, Karen Heuler ("Landscape, With Fish") recalling the time she was levitated, and Matthew Pridham ("Renovations") waxing philosophic on the ineffability of the unseen.

This material comes via a crossover with the "Ecstatic Days" blog of author Jeff VanderMeer, who kindly invited our contributors to appear as his special guest bloggers in December. Look for future installments by Sarah Monette, Norman Spinrad, and more! @

UNDERGROUND THE EXILED ONES WHISPER...

"A clever cocktail that's one part Bulgakov and one part Gaiman — dark, disturbing, audacious, and wry as only a true Russian fantasy can be."

— Gregory Frost
author of *Fitcher's Brides* and *Shadowbridge*

"A jewel of a book, a dispatch from a mythic tradition unfamiliar to most American readers."

— Jay Lake
author of *Mainspring*

"Beautifully nuanced prose . . . a uniquely enchanting fantasy."

— Booklist

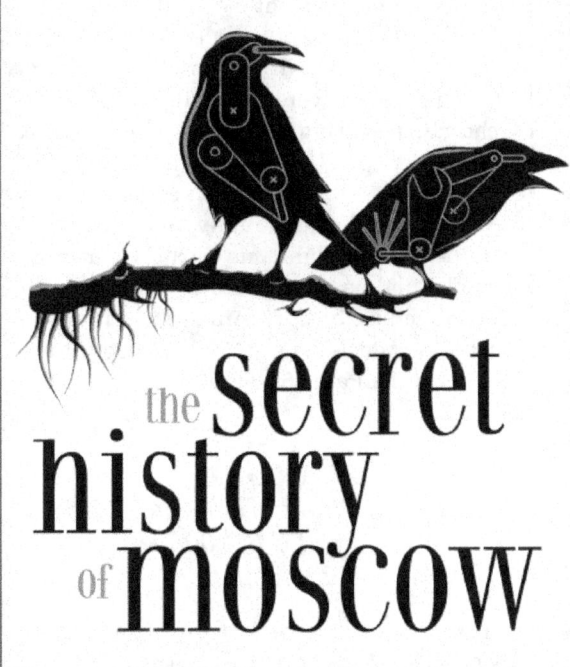

"A lovely, disconcerting book that does for Moscow what I hope my own *Neverwhere* may have done to London."
— NEIL GAIMAN

ekaterina sedia

the secret history of moscow

AVAILABLE NOW IN TRADE PAPERBACK FROM
PRIME BOOKS WHEREVER BOOKS ARE SOLD

Discover more at **www.ekaterinasedia.com**

WEIRD TALES
85TH ANNIVERSARY CALENDAR
Events & Noteworthy Dates in Early 2008

NORWESCON
SeaTac, Washington
March 20-23, 2008
www.norwescon.org

Eighty-five years to the month after the first issue of WEIRD TALES made its debut, we're throwing a party! As it happens, lots of our recent contributing writers live in the Pacific Northwest, so we'll be having a threefold birthday celebration at Norwescon.

First up: a WEIRD TALES retrospective slideshow, on the afternoon of Fri., March 21. Then, that evening, we'll hold a group reading, featuring the likes of Jay Lake, Cherie Priest, Lisa Mantchev, and Ken Scholes, not to mention some contributors from this very issue. Finally, Sat., March 22 will be the big nighttime party. Come mix, mingle, and be on hand to witness the official unveiling of our anniversary issue — including our list of the "85 Weirdest Story-tellers of the Past 85 Years!"

I-CON
SUNY at Stony Brook, New York
April 4-6, 2008
www.iconsf.org

WEIRD TALES fiction editor Ann VanderMeer is an official guest at I-Con, the three-day Long Island festival encompassing a wide range of fantasy, horror, and science fiction, from literature to movies to comics. (The author guest of honor is Charlaine Harris.)

LIBRARY OF CONGRESS
Washington, D.C.
April 11, 2008
www.loc.gov

The Library of Congress's noontime "What If" lecture series will feature editor emeritus George H. Scithers and editorial director Stephen Segal discussing the magazine's illustrious literary and artistic history.

MOCCA ART FESTIVAL
New York, New York
June 7-8, 2008
www.moccany.org

WEIRD TALES will be a media sponsor for the Museum of Comic & Cartoon Art's annual festival at the historic Puck Building in lower Manhattan. Come meet the crew — and discover hundreds of weird new artists!

THE 66TH WORLD SCIENCE FICTION CONVENTION
Denver, Colorado
August 6-10, 2008
www.denvention3.org

"Things to Do in Denver When You're Dead" strikes us as a promising motif. Hmmm: Warren Zevon wrote that song, and Colorado is home to WEIRD TALES contributor Carrie Vaughn, so — whatever we end up doing at Worldcon, expect werewolf involvement . . .

MORE TO BE ANNOUNCED NEXT ISSUE!

Letters

Retroactively Making Monster Motivation

At the end of Erik Amundsen's "Bufo Rex" [issue #347], I was thinking of those old Robert Howard and Lovecraft stories about monstrous old creatures lurking among ruins to be discovered by errant adventurers or inquisitive archeologists, and thought that this would form a marvelous backstory for any one of them. Well done. — *Mike Dominic*

Libidinous Insects Inspire Vocational Pride?

Kurt Newton's "The Release" [issue #344, and also collected in *Weird Tales: The 21st Century, Vol. 1*] is exactly the kind of story that makes me proud to have chosen writing over law. Kudos!
— *Natalie L. Sin*

Black-Magic Fiction Not So Far-Fetched

I loved Natalia Lincoln's "Revival" [issue #341]. I just returned from a trip to the rural South, where I attended a revival-esque funeral service and discovered to my surprise how strong the belief in black magic and mysticism still is among the people there today. Amazing! Thanks for lending a bit of clarity to what I considered at the time to be a rather unconventional funeral service. Great story.
— *Michelle Anderson*

Join the ongoing reader discussion at
WWW.WEIRDTALESMAGAZINE.COM

Weirdism

WALKING WITH THE BEAST

Nonfiction | BY AMANDA GANNON

I T WAS SCARY, being a werewolf's child. My mother was a creative woman with a very animal ability to find delight in the strangest of places. She was fearless and full of adventure. But sometimes she became savage. Then it wasn't hard to see the fur and fangs. Domesticated life in the midwestern suburbs — two kids, two cars, and dinner on the table at seven — didn't suit her. She tried, but it made every day of her life into a struggle against her own nature. Like trapped creatures often do, she lashed out. Sometimes when the pressure became too much she would run away for hours, days at a time. As she grew older, a kind of caged sadness came over her. I never doubted that she loved me, but being her daughter was not easy, especially because I am a werewolf, too.

The signs were there from my first hour. It was a full moon when they cut me from my mother. I was grinning and covered with fine, wolfish hairs. A skittish, quiet, grubby child, I felt more kinship with animals than with other children, and something in me inspired an almost preternatural friendliness in anything carnivorous and furry.

Humanity's strange history gives us tales of feral children raised by wolves, like the wild boy of Aveyron. But there I was, the inverse, something wild raised to be like a human child. To this day I have not lost the habit of growling at strangers or snorting in annoyance. I sniff my friends when I greet them. I have hairy toes. I sleep on the floor.

And no matter how violently I fight against them, I share my mother's violent shifts of mood. I have passed in and out of depression's black forest a dozen times. Between, there are ecstasies where the world seems to bare its throat to me in surrender. I snatch sleep in fitful bursts, fueled for days by a restless energy that spends itself in creativity and aggression. And sometimes, there come terrible fugues when both excitement and despair war within me;

interminable days spent pretending to be human, sleepless nights spent wandering my neighborhood on foot, trying to escape the pain that dogs me.

It is a terrible cycle, its tides compelled not by the moon, but by some inscrutable chemical waxing and waning within the firmament of my brain. And it is crippling. Like my mother, I feel unsuited to this life with its confusing, impossible rules which seem designed to stifle all of my wild joy and which make no provisions for my pain.

At the beginning of my fourth decade, I became dangerous; not to others, but to myself. Thirty years of asking the wrong questions and seeking the wrong solutions had not enabled me to change what I was. I sought help again, resolving to try a final time to try to cure myself, stand upright, and act like a "normal human being."

I did not, of course, acquire a cure. I acquired a diagnosis. The grimoire of the mental health profession is the DSM-IV. It categorises the human soul's many angels and demons — and its beasts. It defines them in human terms, for this human world. And now I can point to my own inner monster, 296.89, Bipolar II Disorder. Quite a pedigree.

All of my failures to shove my hairy emotional paws into humanity's silk slippers were not my fault. My leg-gnawing sorrows are depressions. My frantic moonlight dances with art are a particularly intoxicating variety of hypomania. And my madness, when

I will eventually find myself howling the same madness from the same wild mountaintop.

ILLUSTRATION BY STAR ST. GERMAIN

the two seem hopelessly mingled, are mixed states, and dangerous.

I had always hoped that I would one day grow out of this or be able to outwit it, but now I know that I'm cursed with it forever. No matter how long and far I run, I will eventually find myself back in that same bleak wood, howling the same madness from the same wild mountaintop. In those first days, it felt like all my hope had been kicked into a bottomless hole, dragging the rest of my life in after it. How could I live another fifty years like this?

I didn't want my personality, shaped so much by this thing I am saddled with, to be reduced to nothing more than a constellation of symptoms. My feelings are epic, and no less real for being typical of some illness. The reduction of my essence to a single, inadequate word seemed to reduce me as well.

I felt such terrible shame. Worse than a failure, I was fundamentally flawed.

My husband, who draws me through the worst of the blackness, who sees me at my foaming, animal worst, has never believed in my worthlessness.

"You're not broken," he told me. "You aren't screwed up. You just . . . you are what you are."

"And what am I?" I demanded, because at that point, I honestly didn't know anymore.

"You're a lycanthrope."

"A what?"

"A lycanthrope. You have these . . . episodes. You turn into this beast. But it's a part of you. A perfectly okay part."

Anyone else might have been insulted. Instead, I felt a glimmer of hope. Of course I was not a broken person. I was a werewolf.

Amanda Gannon, a.k.a. Naamah Darling, is an artist and writer who lives in Oklahoma with her husband, Sargon the Terrible, and their menagerie. Her work is online at: **http://naamah-darling.livejournal.com**

My violent mood swings are very much like the unpredictable furies of the horror-movie wolf-man. He cannot control the transformation. In fighting and denying his nature, he lashes out and hurts those closest to him; his beast eventually destroys him because he cannot learn to live with it. I had also rejected my own nature, and now the fear that my beast might destroy me was very real.

I could not cure myself of it any more than it could cure itself of me. We are the same. No, I had to learn to live with it. This chemical rage was more than therapy alone could help. I had tried drugs before, though, and in blocking the path into that black forest, I had also lost the wildness that is the source of my strength. I imagined drugging the beast with antipsychotics and mood stabilizers, thrusting it into a cage again. I imagined it made small, staring numbly out at nothing. There is nothing more pitiable than a wild thing robbed of its wild.

Obviously, I feared treatment as the transfigured wolf-man must fear the silver bullet, but the alternative was letting it spiral out of control until I destroyed myself. Long periods of depression aside, I really do love my life, and so I chose to try drugs rather than risk losing it all — beast, forest, moon and muse, fear, joy, self.

There was still loss. During the months from midsummer to winter's sudden fall I tried and failed and tried again. The first drug physically exhausted me until I couldn't walk around the park. The second strangled all feeling, and I moved in a dead fog. The third undercut my self-control, and I could not function because I could no longer place need above want.

As I write this, six months after my diagnosis, I am on a fourth drug. We are both tolerating it, my beast and I. It gives us the strength to weather the more monstrous shifts of mood, but still allows us to feel. Yes, some days I still feel hollow. Some days there is great pain. But this is a start. I'll never leave this forest, but I believe that I can live here.

I don't believe this because I am an optimist, or because I have read all the right self-improvement books, or because my therapist tells me that I am making progress. I believe it because my bipolar friends are all remarkable, gifted people. Their example reminds me that life as a werewolf is worth living. They are teaching me, at last, to be what I am. They've nicknamed me Wolfchild, and though any mental disorder is by nature isolating, I have seen that we all roam the same forest. We are lone wolves, but our paths cross, our songs reach one another.

I also have many friends who are not bipolar, and they have not run from me; they are at peace with my wildness and they do not want me tame.

Werewolf and human alike, they share their poems and their pictures and their stories and their lives to show me what is possible, what is best in both sides of my nature.

My mother was never diagnosed as bipolar, though the signs were there. She died without knowing she was a werewolf. Perhaps . . . perhaps if she'd known, she would have lived a better life not in a cage of her own making. I hope that is true of me. Knowing what I am saves me from trying to be what I thought I should have been. I am not trying to fix a broken person, I am learning to live as a healthy werewolf. I am not there yet, but I have found a little acceptance.

Most nights I leave the house and wander on foot down familiar streets. I listen to the highway's roar and the howl of distant trains. The familiar stink of garbage, car exhaust, of leaves and wet pavement surround me. Sometimes the trees wave in the wind and their shadows bound in the streetlights' sodium glare, and for a moment this human city seems wild. I feel the beast stir deep within me, and my humanity lays down beside it. In those moments I am filled with something that I cannot name. I feel on the verge of becoming what I was meant to be.

That's the big lycanthropic secret: that no matter how terrible, being what you are can be beautiful. ☉

A MORBID PROPOSAL

Ideas | BY JEREMIAH TOLBERT

S O I'VE BEEN spending my spare time trying to hook up the Internet to the afterlife. Why? Because it's going to make me rich. Here's how:

The afterlife is just one big gray mess. Remember that part in *The Odyssey* where Odysseus visits the underworld, and everyone wants to talk to him? It's exactly like that. A bunch of bored dead people with absolutely nothing to do but wail about *how* bored they are and bicker with one another. Basically, the dead are exactly like teenagers before they get their driver's licenses.

Giving the afterlife Internet will probably hurt things at first, I'll admit. We'll be looking at a flood of computer idiots that will make the early days of AOL joining the Web look like nothing in comparison. Lots of angry, whiny posts. Blogger and LiveJournal servers will probably go down from all the new account sign-ups. Inevitably, the dead will discover porn, which means they'll need to earn money to pay for the porn sites . . . which means they'll turn to spam. Your inbox will fill up with offers to put you in touch with your lost loved ones, secret hypnotic techniques of the ancient Egyptians — that kind of thing. But eventually, after some spam-filter retraining, things will calm down.

So how's this going to make me rich? Well, I'm a Web designer. There are going to be certain ex-famous members of the dead who'll want to set the record straight. It's assholes and opinions: everyone has one. (Although I guess the dead don't have assholes anymore.) So I'm going to build websites for the wronged dead. I'm thinking, I'll start with former politicians and pirates. Why? Buried treasure. In exchange for giving them a voice on the Web, they're going to tell me where they hid the loot.

I'm telling you, this plan is foolproof. Now if you'll excuse me, I need to go ping Hades. I think I've almost managed to get TCP/IP to pierce the Veil. ☺

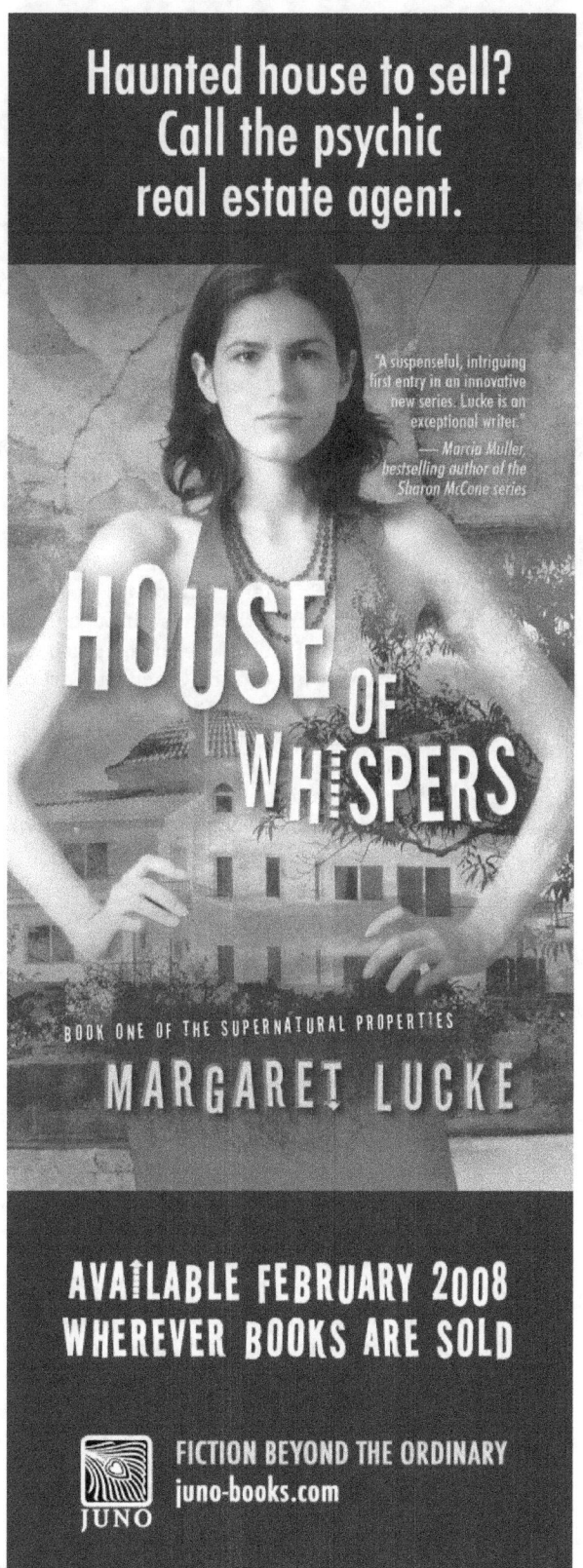

The Library

A DEN OF INFINITY

HAVOC SWIMS JADED
by David J. Schow
(Subterranean Press, $25)

It's been said of Poe that no sooner had he invented the detective story than he abandoned it. The same thing might well be said for David Schow and "splatterpunk," the literary subgenre he helped invent during the "horror boom" of the 1980s. Splatterpunk attempts to elicit a visceral reaction from the reader through the graphic depiction of violence — an approach that harkens back at least to the Grand Guignol of Paris and the *conte cruel*. But just as there is more to Robert Bloch (an author whose work Schow continues to champion) than *Psycho*, Schow's work cannot be neatly pigeonholed into any single category. In a 2003 interview with *Publishers Weekly*, he went as far as to state that what he is most proud of regarding splatterpunk is that it earned him an entry in the Oxford English Dictionary for coining the phrase.

Schow's most recent collection, *Havoc Swims Jaded*, sports a title whose significance is apparently deliberately obscure and selected mostly (if not entirely) for its disquieting qualities. Disquieting is indeed the proper word to describe the fourteen stories that make up this collection. It gets off to a running start with what purports to be an editorial written for a fictional magazine by one "Bertrand Nightenhelser," a jeremiad against conventionality and commercialism in horror publishing and ends up as a paranoid rambling whose chilling significance only becomes apparent in a footnote. This sort of indirect approach is a hallmark of Schow's work, who demonstrates that he >>>

Two Resurrections from Classic WT Author Clark Ashton Smith

Donald Sidney-Fryer's classic biographical-critical studio **The Sorcerer Departs: Clark Ashton Smith (1893-1961)** has been reprinted in a new, corrected edition by the French publisher Silver Key Press (http://silverkeypress.free.fr) for the munificent sum of ten euros, postage included. This is still the single best introduction to Smith's work.

The late California bookseller Roy A. Squires was a friend of Smith who served as his literary executor for a while. He owned a private press that produced several chapbooks by Smith that were set on handmade paper from handset type; these are among the most sought-after items for Smith collectors. Now Squires' friend and heir Terence McVicker (mcrarebooks@earthlink.net) has revived Squires' press for the 20th anniversary of its last production. **The Black Abbot of Puthuum** is the first publication of the longer, original version of this tale of Zothique, which had been cut and edited for its March 1936 WEIRD TALES appearance. This rather hefty 44-page chapbook was designed by Gerald Lange of The Bieler Press, and is printed on Mohawk 50/10 Matte and Curtis Flannel; each of the 250 numbered copies is hand-sewn into its covers. Laid in is a reproduction of Virgil Finlay's illustration for the story. At $49.95 it is not cheap, but it is a worthwhile tribute to one of Smith's greatest champions that will surely be a sought-after collector's item. — *S.C.*

>>> can do the sort of "twisting-the-knife" endings for which Bloch was renowned. "The Absolute Last of the Ultra-Spooky, Super-Scary Hallowe'en Horror Nights" deals with the unconventional response a theme park has developed in dealing with would-be vandals out to spoil their Hallowe'en programming. "Expanding Your Capabilities Using Frame/Shift™ Mode" is an ingenious and ironic look at how technology shapes how we react to reality—and perhaps how reality reacts to us. "The Five Sisters: A Fable" and "The Thing Too Hideous To Describe" are perhaps too unsubtle in their didacticism and strike me as being atypical. "Plot Twist" is a more successful example of Schow's experimental writing; this tale of three friends stranded in the desert really takes the proverbial "left turn at Albuquerque" and provides exactly what the title promises, and then some.

Schow continues to prove himself one of the genre's finest stylists, selecting precisely the right word for the situation described so that its emotional impact on the reader is maximized. In fact, each of the stories in this collection, the author's seventh, manages to subvert the reader's expectations in a manner that ratchets up the impact of the denouement by at least an order of magnitude. — *Scott Connors*

THE LEAGUE OF EXTRAORDINARY GENTLEMEN: BLACK DOSSIER
by Alan Moore and Kevin O'Neill
(America's Best Comics, $29.99)

Alan Moore's *The League of Extraordinary Gentlemen: Black Dossier* is either an extended gimmick or a work of genius, depending on how you look at it. Skim the hardcover and you'll experience ever so briefly the extended prose sections, feel the changing paper stock, and even catch a glimpse of the tipped-in "Tijuana bible" before flipping to the end and seeing the 3-D glasses taped to the back cover flap. Gimmick.

However, if you sit down and closely read *Black Dossier*, you will be won over. The first two volumes of the *League* were clever: Mina Harker, Allan Quatermain, Edward Hyde, Captain Nemo, and the Invisible Man square off again Fu Manchu and the tripods of Mars. There

were innumerable references in both the text and art to literary characters both high and low, to the extent where a book of annotations was published. But if the first *League* volumes were just goofy riffs on classic pulp characters, *Black Dossier* is Coltrane and Miles Davis. Genius.

Black Dossier is the story of Harker and the recently rejuvenated Quatermain appropriating the titular dossier from the post-1948 Big Brother government (and under the nose of a young James Bond!) as well as being the dossier itself. Memoirs of Fanny Hill; intelligence reports of the French and German analogs to the League (featuring Doctor Caligari, Fantomas, and others); and an excerpt of "Sal Paradyse's" *The Crazy Wide Forever*, in which Harker and Quatermain confront "Doctor Sachs" at the dawn of the Beat era are just a few of the pieces of the dossier presented with an eye toward the telling detail. *Black Dossier* isn't just a history of comics and pulp fiction, but of design and printing technologies. It isn't just fiction either — one pieces together the extended history of the League as it played out both before and after the initial two volumes of the comic in the way one might reconstruct one's grandparents' lives from their old letters, bank books, family photos, and legal papers. Carnacki makes an appearance, so do an Elder God or too, and the Orwellian disclaimer at the beginning of the dossier — THIS WARN YOU — is worth the price alone.

Like any long jazz jam, there are a few bum notes. Moore's attempt at nucleic exchange between Wodehouse and Lovecraft isn't nearly so amusing as Peter H. Cannon's *Scream for Jeeves*, and the framing story doesn't really get hot until Bulldog Drummond and Emma Peel from *The Avengers* show up. Finally, maybe my nose is too big, but the 3-D glasses were a tight fit, and thus the final pages in which the dossier is handed off to Prospero in the extradimensional Blazing World made me dizzy. These are all minor complaints. *Black Dossier* is so rich in text, art, and design, and fully comprehending it requires such an expansive synoptic facility – or at least long nights of Googling — that you won't read it. You'll refer to it, over and over, dipping in like you would into a collection of jazz LPs. — *Nick Mamatas*

WICKED LOVELY

MELISSA MARR ON FOLKLORE & TATTOOS

INTERVIEW BY ELIZABETH GENCO

To brazenly steal from a certain TV infomercial which shall remain nameless: I'm not just a writer of mythic fiction, I'm also a devotee. So when I stumbled on Melissa Marr's LiveJournal late one night, I quickly added her to my friends list so that I might watch her story unfold. In addition to exciting publishing-biz tales — review copies! foreign editions! — Melissa talked openly about her relationship with her muse: "Ms. Muse," to be specific.

Melissa's devotion to Ms. Muse has paid off in spades. Her first novel, Wicked Lovely, has received far too many accolades to mention here. The next book in the series, Ink Exchange, hits the shelves in late April 2008; we've got a third book and a manga series from Tokyopop to look forward to in 2009.

Almost as impressive as Melissa's prose is the speed with which it reached mass audiences. After some "starts of a novel" in 2004, her journey from *first page to* New York Times *bestseller list (Wicked Lovely debuted at No. 8) was about two years. Melissa recently sat down with* WEIRD TALES *to discuss the cauldron of ideas and influences that helps to fuel her work.*

Your next book, *Ink Exchange,* **is about faeries and tattoos. When did you get your first tattoo?** In my mid-20s, I picked my artist. I wanted an ivy vine and 6 white lilies. The vine was to be encircling my torso. My artist refused to do a large project on virgin skin, so my first session was just a pair of white lilies on my sternum. Afterwards, I affirmed that I still wanted the rest, so he gave me my vine and lilies over the next few months. That was about ten years ago. There have been a few tattoos between then and now, and I'm currently getting the ivy re-touched (to brighten it) and adding more branches.

Tell me a bit about your relationship with folklore. How and when did it reel you in? I grew up believing in faeries, ghosts, vampires, and shapeshifters. These weren't creatures in another realm though. They walked here. The Wild Hunt was as likely as not to be thundering by as one walked home from the pub . . . or so my family told me.

Was belief in the Otherworld a big part of your family's culture? For a number of family members, yes, belief was just the way of it. Supposedly, there were psychics in the family tree (possibly something with a carnival, the details were always vague). There were dishes left for the Good Neighbors. What some might call superstition was normal. I remember a relative going out gathering herbs in the woods. Those were from both sides of the family.

The story goes that all the relatives on both sides came from Ireland or Scotland — except one from Germany. My Great-Grandmother Rose was an Irish citizen who spoke Irish/Gaelic. The rest? Did I mention the

storytelling tradition? Answers are fluid sometimes. "He was Irish, by way of Scotland. No, no! He was Scottish." This one changed his name because he had some "troubles" attached to that name. That one claimed to be from there because of a "misunderstanding with the lawman." It's not the truth but the tale that matters. But as best as I can understand, there's relatives from Ireland, Scotland, and Germany. Luckily for me, all three are rich in storytelling, folklore, and fairytales.

Between this belief system and a pile of books in my Gramma's house, I guess I always believed. As I got older, I read more and more books. I still do.

You are very open in interviews about being a "muse writer." What are your favorite ways to court Ms. Muse? I don't do favorites, per se. I've never been good at picking just one of anything. The frequent ones have been going to museums, oceans, desert, listening to music, getting tattooed, roaming aimlessly with my camera and meditating. It's about sating my senses or trying to fill my spirit. Sometimes it's also about letting the body be distracted so the text can simmer in the subconscious level. Often, I believe, we know the next bit of a tale, but we are trying so hard to reach it that we are blocking ourselves. My solution is to argue that the not-at-the-desk part is a critical part of the process rather than trying to force ourselves into some regimented structure.

Very, very wise. Also easier said than done, I find — it's like I've internalized the pressure of the world-at-large to Always Be Productive. It comes down to how you define "productive," though. Without caution, I'm a hardcore workaholic, so I must force myself to remember that what we feed in determines what we can do. How is one to write without pausing to live? It's not easy to find the time, but a few hours of "muse feeding" does wonders for the text.

For example, I was just out on tour again (the second one HarperCollins sent me on for this first book), and there weren't many free hours in the schedule. Still, I took 90 minutes to walk around a botanical garden in Phoenix, an hour to roam the streets of Chicago, and a bit of time to go to the Dali Museum in Florida. It wasn't much, and I suspect that sleep would've been useful in those same windows, but those hours in those places all fuel the words I will write.

Creativity is tied to chaos and randomness for me, so I indulge my whims. It's more fun, and it seems to be working just fine.

I found this great interview where you talk about the revision process for *Wicked Lovely*. And that got me thinking about a favorite question. Are you a swooper or a banger? (Swoopers swoop in and just get it all out onto the paper, overwriting and making massive edits later. Bangers carefully craft each word, banging out each sentence before moving on to the next.) Can I pick hybrid? I think it depends on the text. Sometimes I think I have a process, but each text has been a little different. I don't know that I'd ever want to say "A-ha! I do it this way" because then it would be predictable, which would lead to boredom, which is bad for me. Writing is still a new adventure without a clear process. As long as it stays this way, I think I'll be able to do it for a while.

You've bartended, taken road trips, been a teacher, and have done all sorts of cool things. Name something you have yet to do but would like to do. Everyone's done interesting things; that's part of why I like talking to people — to learn about their experiences. I don't have any set thing I'm craving above all others. I just hope that I'll continue giving in to stray urges. I recently offered to be a receptionist at a tattoo convention. I don't think they'll agree, but I'm still hopeful.

"Creativity is tied to chaos and randomness for me, so I indulge my whims."

How could they not agree? What's to say no to? The challenge is trying to convince the people at the booth I volunteered for that they *need* a receptionist. Granted, I could go and just roam, but I love trying new jobs or new functions. I've never worked at a booth *or* been a receptionist, so I really want to. I've offered to deal with paperwork, fetch coffee, whatever. I have a "maybe" answer so far, but I'm going to keep trying!

Most of my jobs I took on a whim — including the first bartending job. There are so many experiences I haven't had yet. I don't ever want to get to the point where I feel like I've missed the chance to live. ℮

The most direct way to relate to your madness is to think of it as a 'stone' in your head. Other analogies include a 'flower'* but either way, the condition is certainly quite off putting. If one hopes to establish a reputable social presence, no measure can be seen as unorthodox. The stone must be cracked.

BEING·MINDFUL·OF·YOUR·MADNESS
with the Angel Interceptor

Since the decline of leprosy in the Middle Ages, madness came to occupy the position of 'most unfavorable trait' in Western culture. With many an article in popular journals, the general public is very attuned to detecting the '3 of Insanity'. Rank yourself in severity.

WILD EYE
1 2 3 4 5

JELLY LEG
1 2 3 4 5

FURY HAND
1 2 3 4 5

*·From which the insult 'tulip head' emerges.

FINDING A CURE

I
t is likely you live in a region of an oppressive hegemonic culture where the phenomenon of mental illness is believed to be 'a fragile condition.' An egg, not a stone. Naturally one chooses to be pampered instead of brutalized, but consider this scenario:
You have contracted pneumonia and the fastest cure is a session in a head vice. Do you refuse? No, you do not. Here are more economical treatments.

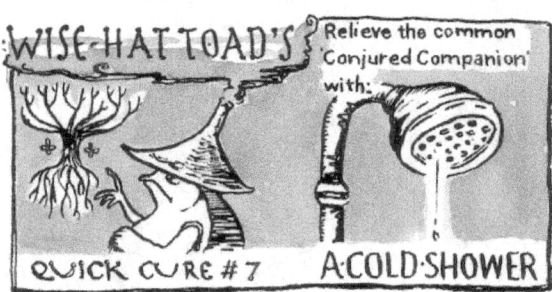

WISE-HAT TOAD'S

Relieve the common 'Conjured Companion' with:

QUICK CURE #7 — A COLD SHOWER

Blood-letting is a simple, and at times, effective method of therapy. Gathering the following tools.

- DILATING STICK*
- TOURNIQUET
- TRANSFUSION (Sheep/Horse)

blood

*-Inspiration for Barber's Pole.

THE TOM RAKEWELL CLINIC
"Raising bars since 1878"

"We have made a commitment to beat lunacy together."

Fig.L

"Each patient will be subjected to our most effective methods, no matter the severity of their condition. There is nothing to gain by analyzing a fallacious mind. Really, nothing at all."

BY IRA MARCKS

Brief Glimpses of Another World

BY F.J. BERGMANN

1.

It flew right up my nose, which is probably
somebody's idea of a good time.
With an unpopular orifice.
I was hoping it would remember
to turn off the lights.

2.

You can't judge a book by its spread or a bed
by its cover. That was my skin,
thank you so very much.
Some people have this thing
about transgression.

3.

If it's blue it's not food. If it's yellow
it's probably not toothpaste,
not that I would presume to give you
advice, at least not for free. Much as
it pains me to mention it.

4.

I don't do push-ups because I'm not insecure
about my physique. My credit rating,
yes. If you thought I was going
to discuss my underwear,
you can just forget it.

5.

It was up in the tree again, and the firemen
said it probably lived there.
The rent is free, but doesn't
include utilities. Even so,
there's a waiting list.

6.

She said she was a career girl until she was
de-pleated (lost her skirt, baton-twirling).
She was a very professional
drum majorette
for the March of Dimes.

7.

Don't you just love those interactive books
where you choose how the plot
will thicken? Or curdle. I go for
the idea of alternative endings,
especially for the 1040-EZ.

The House of Idiot Children

BY W.H. PUGMIRE & M.K. SNYDER

ILLUSTRATED BY NIGEL SADE

IN WHICH
LANGUAGE IS NOT
A VIRUS FROM
OUTER SPACE,
EXACTLY

SAMUEL SHAMMUA WATCHED the tree coming toward him just in time to avoid collision. True, the moist fog had been thick, limiting visibility; and true, the road curved endlessly, making navigation treacherous. Yet truest of all was the inescapable fact that Samuel had been dreaming, that he had not been paying attention to the little of the road that had spread visibly before his bicycle. And thus his vehicle had run off the road onto an area of grass, and thus he had to put on the brakes and slid to a sudden stop before smashing into an elder oak.

"Oy," he muttered, hearing again the scolding inner-voice, that sound of reproof that was forever condemning and condescending. "Always with your head in the clouds, like already you were in the next world." He ignored the voice and got off the old bike. The cheder was just around the bend, better he should stroll than pedal. So walk he did, until he entered the lush woodland property that surrounded the ancient wooden edifice that had, almost one century before, served as secluded temple for a fledgling Jewish community, until most of its congregates had moved so as to settle in a section of town that was more suitable to an increase of prosperity. Thus the building served as Hebrew school, until even that proved unfeasible. Still, the community loved the building and could not sell it to the goyim who showed an interest in it; and thus it became a school for children who were autistic, a place that instituted a radical program of learning by facilitation.

Parking his bike, Samuel wiped moisture from his face, and then looked to an upper window, where he saw a figure waving at him. The pane of glass was thick with a residue of mist, yet the figure of his student, Moshe, was clearly identifiable. Shocked and delighted at the sight, Samuel raised his hand in greeting; and then it became clear that the boy was not waving at him but rather pressing fingers against the window's fog and writing a Hebrew letter. Samuel watched, astounded, and then confused, for the letter written was oddly formed, resembling a mish-mash combination of different characters of the alphabet. The misty image of the autistic child took its hand from the pane of glass, and then began to bow toward the letter, as if in prayer. A chill crept Samuel's spine as the malformed letter began to subtly glow, as if suddenly hit with ethereal light. Turning, the teacher scanned the skies, yet saw no speck of sunlight filtering through the density of fog. When again he looked at the window, Moshe and the illuminated letter were no longer there.

He climbed the steps that led to an expansive porch, kissed fingers that touched the slightly ornate mezuzah, his fingertips lingering just beneath the opening wherein the name of God, Shaddai, was written on the back of the klaf, the rolled parchment on which the Shema prayer from Deuteronomy 6 had been handwritten. Softly, he spoke the prayer, elongating the pronunciation of the final "d" in "echad". Then he pushed open

the door and entered the building, smiling greeting as Rebbe Paloy approached him.

"Ah, Rav Samuel," the old man enthused, holding out his hands in greeting, one of which grasped a sheet of paper. Beaming excitedly, he held the paper before Samuel's face. "This is remarkable."

Samuel waited until the paper was placed within his hands. He saw that it was the poem that his student had written in English two days previously. The English of the verse was awkward, but the composition of the poem itself had been an exciting milestone in Moshe's progress. "Yes, Rebbe, it is exciting."

The elder gentleman's eyes twinkled magically. He held a finger before Samuel's nose. "Aha," the Rebbe said, almost laughing the word, and then he reached into a pocket and produced another sheet of paper. "This is my Hebrew translation of the poem. What do you make of it?" Samuel studied the Hebrew letters and thought it a fine translation. Before him, the old man was fidgeting with anticipation. "Nu? Do you notice anything? "The Rebbe watched impatiently as Samuel frowned in concentration. Then the old man shrugged and took back the sheet of paper. "You were never so good with numbers, eh, Rav Samuel? The gematria of this poem is spectacular. You see? Every line reduces to nine."

Samuel scanned the sheet held before him again, frowning in confusion. "Rebbe, the poem was written in English."

Again, the Rebbe's significant finger poked the air before Samuel's nose. "Aha!"

"But that would mean that Moshe mentally composed the poem in Hebrew, then wrote it out in his awkward English translation!"

"Aha!"

Samuel shook his dazed head. "I don't know what to say."

The Rebbe shrugged. "Say nothing. What's to say? Your student awaits you." And with a triumphal air, the old man strode away, chuckling to himself.

Slowly, thoughtfully, Samuel climbed the stairs that took him to one of the upper facilitation rooms. The door to his room of destination was open, and looking in he saw two tables where students and teachers were at work. His heart filled with sudden tenderness at the sight, at how tenderly the teachers held their students hands, at how gently the students nodded their heads as they spoke by way of assisted writing. There was something sacred in the sight, he felt this deeply. In a corner, at a table near to a window, sat his student, with feathery fair hair escaping from beneath a yarmulke. Samuel walked to the silent child.

"Hello, Moshe."

"Hello, Rav Samuel," came the boy's thick voice, from a face that did not acknowledge him. Samuel sat next to the boy; felt as he always did that Moshe was a special creature, one of the elect. And then he felt a twinge of guilt, for it was important in this school not to treat the students as if they were anything but normal. Gently, Samuel took a sheet of paper from a small stack and placed it before his student, then tenderly placed a pencil in Moshe's hand. Lovingly, he took hold of his student's hands, then closed his eyes and offered up a silent prayer. The hands began to move, from right to left. Opening his eyes, Samuel saw a verse from Isaiah that they had been studying being written in Hebrew. He nodded and smiled; and then he suddenly frowned as the hands ceased their movement, except for a slight trembling.

He raised his eyes to look at the face of his student and saw the boy's nodding head turned to the nearby window, from which a misty light filtered into the room. The light altered, transforming in hue, became a lustrous entity. A particle of this illumination detached itself and drifted to them, floated to Moshe's mouth and touched his slightly moving lips. Silently, the boy sighed a sound that was almost heard by his teacher, a sound that was felt in the pit of his being. The patch of light rested on the sheet of paper, paper that was now of brilliant whiteness. Filled with sudden terror, Samuel watched joined hands move toward and into the light, watched as the pencil held in Moshe's grasp move swiftly and form what at first seemed to be a Hebrew letter, but one that was unfamiliar. Samuel stared at the alien glyph, this thing that seemed more symbol than character of alphabet. Samuel studied the amazing thing and realized that it was an ambigram, a symbol that is exactly the same read backward, forward, upside-down. The Star of David was such a symbol, as was the yin yang, or the runic swastika. Trembling, Samuel bent to the symbol so as to better study it, then released Moshe's hand and touched the shimmering symbol. Eyesight blurred, and ice water surged through his veins. Soft lips touched his ear and breathed into him an alien sound that his brain could not perceive or replicate. Heavily, Rav Samuel tilted from the table and fell heavily to the floor.

II.

REBECCA SHAMMUA BENT over her garden, tending to a cluster of daffodils that fought for space among the pale petals of the poet's narcissus, and the gorgeous red and white flowers of the few amaryllis that she had added for a contrast of color. Her long free-flowing hair touched the blossoms, and lines from Dante Gabriel Rossetti came to mind:

She had three lilies in her hand,

And the stars in her hair were seven.

How wonderful, she thought, for a poet to have as part of his bi-line the name of an archangel, an angel of fire. She had seen several Christian representations of Gabriel, in which he held in his hand a lily rather than a sword. As she knelt, lost in thought, a cloud moved away from the sun, and celestial fire crowned her head. Lifting her eyes to the sun, she squinted momentarily at its glory; and then her eyes took in the figure that shambled toward her, the human outline that was blurred by the glare of bright light that had been caught inside her eyes.

Dimly, she made him out, the young man with the boyish beginning of a beard, whose dark haunted eyes peered from a face of extremely pale flesh.

Her brother knelt next to her, smiling at her petulant frown. "Why are you out of bed? Are you hungry?"

"Food is your answer to all the ills of life," Samuel laughed.

"Food is a gift from Hashem, and a blessing for our bellies."

Samuel paused in thought, trying to remember if this was a Rabbinical saying or merely his younger sister being womanly wise. "I've yet to eat. But I am getting hungry." Abstractedly, he smoothed fingers to the small bump on his head.

"How are you feeling, really? Yes, I'm worried; of course I am, having you brought home in such a state. A fainting spell! Why would you faint, unless you're forgetting to eat?"

"I didn't faint from not eating, Rebecca. I eat plenty. No, I . . . " He stopped to think back on the events of the previous day, absentmindedly playing in the dirt with his small finger. He tried to remember his fainting spell, but could not. Everything was like a memory of a dream, his teaching Moshe, his weird accident, those who helped him home. Turning to smile at his sister, he was struck by the odd expression on her face. She was watching intently the movement of his hand. Looking down at the dirt in which he played, he saw that he had been forming letters in the fine sod.

Soothingly, her hand covered his. "What are you doing?"

"I . . . I . . . " And suddenly the sod turned cold, like chilly funeral earth. He studied the odd semi-letters he had written, letters that looked like a child's attempt at first forming members of the Hebrew alphabet, letters that almost looked correct, yet contained odd mistakes, queer additions. Swiftly, he took his hand out of the dirt and struggled to his feet, wobbling for a moment. Fearing that he was having another fainting spell, Rebecca

shot to her feet with a cry and held him tightly in her arms. Samuel trembled in her embrace, unable to decipher the element of fear and wonder that filled his soul.

"I'm fine," he tried to reassure her, in a voice that belied his statement. Slowly, they returned to the house, and he sat at the kitchen table and watched as she prepared a meal. "How is Mother?" he asked as a plate was placed before him.

"Still sleeping, probably. I'll check on her after you've eaten. Eat, eat!" And she sat next to him, with a plate of her own, until a knocking at the front door took her from the kitchen. When she returned, Rebbe Paloy accompanied her, smiling his calm smile.

He thanked Rebecca as she placed a cup of hot tea before him, reached into a small bowl and took from it a sugar cube which he placed inside his mouth. Thoughtfully, he sipped from the teacup.

"You are feeling better, Rav Samuel?"

"Yes, Rebbe, I feel fine, merely confused. I'm not prone to fainting spells."

"It wasn't nice. Little Moshe was very upset."

"I'm very sorry that it happened. I can't explain it."

Shrugging, the old man reached into a coat pocket and brought forth a folded sheet of paper. He set it on the table before them and slowly opened it, watching closely the strange expression on the younger fellow's face. Samuel watched as the Rebbe's fingers traced the Hebrew verse of Isaiah that had been clumsily written. The finger stopped at a place on the paper that was faintly discolored, looking slightly scorched. The elder man watched, fascinated, as Samuel touched the spot of discolored paper, watched as Samuel's dark eyes seemed almost to grow pale with memory and emotion. "Can you explain this?" asked the Rebbe, his finger gently touching Samuel's.

"I . . . it . . . " the younger man stammered. "It defies explanation. It appeared out of a cloud of fire."

The Rebbe's friendly finger tapped

Samuel's. "Like Ezekiel and his cherubim? Of the nine classes of angels, they are most associated with fire and lightning. Nu, are you becoming a prophet, Samuel?" He lightly laughed, and winked at Rebecca's worried face. She brought another plate of food to the Rebbe.

"I must go check on Mother, Samuel. Forgive me, Rebbe."

"Go, go," he pleasantly answered, nodding at the sandwich that he held before happy eyes. The eyes slid to look at Samuel. "Nu?"

"No, not an angel," the young man finally spoke, quietly and to himself. "It was a letter, or a queer combination of portions of different letters, and it contained a quality of light. It seemed so real. It seemed almost to beckon, as though it longed for adoration."

Rebbe Paloy was silent for a moment. "And where did you see this? Was it a Hebrew letter?"

"Moshe wrote it — there." And he tapped the discolored spot.

"A twenty-third Hebrew letter, a letter of fire." The elder man raised his hand so as to thoughtfully stroke his beard. "An angelic letter. A letter out of which nothing is formed."

Samuel's face felt odd, and he ran his hands over it, trying not to shudder. "You know of this?" His voice was laced with fear, for never had he experienced such a conversation. The mysteries of kabalistic lore were something with which he had never trafficked. He had seen certain friends of his become utterly obsessed with studying the Zohar and other such books, to the detriment of everything else. It was a lure in which he had no wish to find himself entangled. He was a teacher; he had a duty to his students, to Moshe. Whatever this thing was, it had nothing whatsoever to do with him.

"The creator used the alphabet to form the worlds, this one and the world to come. When we study Torah, when we speak the holy language, we help to recreate the world. There are worlds of substance, of which we are eternally a part. And then, maybe, there are the realms of naught. Realms formed of nothing, from an alphabet of nothingness."

"I've never heard of such a thing."

"Well," the Rebbe laughed, eyes twinkling, "it's not something one learns about in cheder. And I do not think it is something we should dwell on. You will return to work tomorrow, yes?"

Quietly, Rebecca returned into the room and watched expectantly as the Rebbe, groaning, rose to his feet. Samuel didn't watch as they left the room together, his mind too preoccupied with uncanny thought. Thus he did not see as his sister anxiously whispered to the Rebbe as she escorted him from the kitchen.

III.

SAMUEL PARKED HIS bike and anxiously looked up at the window where he had seen Moshe the previous day. No one stood there, watching. He walked into the building, greeted by anxious smiles. He sensed that he had been the topic of conversation, because of his unexpected fainting spell. He knew that the Rebbe would never relate the source of that peculiar experience with the other teachers. He walked into the classroom and saw some students who, sitting at various tables, were awaiting their instructors. They sat there, some very still, some moving slightly back and forth, all staring into the air before them. Samuel shocked himself by feeling suddenly jealous. What did they see as they looked into nothingness. What did they listen to with an inner ear? The world saw these children as idiots who would always have difficulty functioning with the normal ear; and yet these children each contained a singular degree of genius. One was a mathematic genius. Another had memorized huge portions of Torah and Talmud in both English and Hebrew. And Moshe, who sat awaiting him, had excelled in the art of gematria, which art had so excited the

Rebbe, but which would have little importance in everyday experience.

He went to the table and silently sat next to the child. He seemed almost afraid to utter sound. Placing a sheet of paper before the boy, he placed a pencil in the child's hand, and then began the ritual of facilitation. He watched his student's face as Moshe's hand moved the pencil over the paper. The boy's face was bland, except for a slight twitching of the mouth. The eyes seemed dull, lacking of even the idea of thought or communication. Once again, Samuel wondered at the world wherein this child's mind was encased. What did the dull eyes see? What sounds flowed within the skull's space? How wonderful it would be if he, Samuel, the man of sophistication and intellect, could experience the realm of idiocy. He keenly longed for such a skill. When at last he looked down at the words written onto paper, he was startled to see a poem, written in awkward English. Softly, he spoke the words:

> *Do you hear singing in the head?*
> *Pounding like ocean in ears.*
> *Scream like pain, on fire with color.*
> *The color on fire, the cold fire?*
> *Fire of pain behind your eyes*
> *Burns in place where you are not autistic.*
> *Like everyone, normal, like man who*
> *holds your hand.*

The boy beside him was silent, swaying slightly to and fro. "What is this, Moshe?"

"Poem," the boy muttered.

"And where do you see this cold fire?" he asked, although he intuited that he was entering a dangerous place, a place forbidden.

"In my eyes. It burns my eyes, and then I see."

"What do you see?"

The child began to slightly shiver, then leaned so that he touched his head to Samuel's. Dry lips touched Samuel's ears, and cool air pushed into that cavity of sound. A word was whispered, just below the sound of whispering. It was an idiotic sound, phrased as only autistic lips could speak it. Samuel's brain refused to take it in, to understand it. He could not comprehend the spoken sound. It was too unearthly. Cool air breathed into his ear, air that seemed almost to burn his brain, and once more a sound was whispered. It echoed inside him, a reverberation that he could almost taste, could almost see. His tingling lips parted, and a whisper slipped from out his mouth. But something in the sound frightened him, and he forced himself to his feet, away from the boy who wore no expression, the child who subtly swayed as if in time to a song that only he could hear. One hand still held a pencil, the point of which tapped fitfully onto a sheet of paper. Samuel looked around him and saw other facilitators staring at him with worried faces. Smiling, he calmed his nerves and returned to his chair, onto which he lightly sat. With fingers that slightly trembled, he took hold of Moshe's hands and began the ritual of facilitation.

It was a holy ritual, and a gentle one. The boy beside him was a vessel, a ferry to a spiritual plane that Samuel could not comprehend. Tender bones moved beneath Moshe's thin fabric of skin, and delicate muscles pushed the pencil across bright paper. "Concentrate on your pupil," Samuel silently chided himself. "Step out of dreaming and do your job."

The workday ended, and the students returned to the rooms that were their temporary homes. Samuel stepped outside so as to watch the late afternoon sky throw its misty light through branches and leaves. Sensing that someone was watching him, Samuel turned and saw another facilitator, Avram, smiling at him. After an awkward hesitation, the other man approached. Samuel watched the play of light and shadow that moved on Avram's face as he walked beneath the silent trees.

"How are you feeling, Samuel? No more fainting spells?"

"I'm fine, Avram. A little tired, perhaps."

"Exhausted by your genius, no doubt. He's a handful, your Moshe. Excelling in gematria now, whoo. I didn't know you dabbled in Kabbalah."

Samuel lightly laughed. "I never have. When I was a kid our Rabbi warned us against the enticing of esoteric lore. The mysteries were not for us, but for the elect or the slightly loony. I had a friend who became obsessed with the Zohar, and in later life he had to be institutionalized. He was a genius, a raving genius. Such brilliance can be rather terrifying." Something warned him to not speak of these things, not to trust his fellow facilitator. He found that he did not want to share the topic of Moshe with anyone. "How goes it with your little Joshua?"

"Very slowly. I sometimes get impatient, want to coax, as we are reputed to do."

"Feh," Samuel spat. "I was paired with Moshe because of my standing as amateur poet. Moshe showed poetic ability, and so we became a team. This other stuff is far beyond me. It's for Hashem to understand and direct. Our critics, who say that we influence our pupils, consciously or unconsciously, should mind their own business."

"They don't want parents to become overly encouraged when these kids begin to seem more — more like others."

"They're not like others, that's the point!" Samuel suddenly shouted, his face flushed with anger. "They are special creatures, for whom we especially care. What the hell is normal, Avram? Were you a normal kid? Our religious and ethnic heritage makes us outsiders in the normal world, that's why we're hated, that's why madmen seek to destroy us."

"I'm sorry, Samuel. Please, settle down."

Samuel shut his eyes and fought to control his breathing. He smiled, and then began to laugh. "It's been a long day. Yes? Forgive me, I'm tired. Listen, come eat with us. Halibut, as only my sister can bake it. Talk about esoteric knowledge. Come, Avram, it's been weeks since you've visited my sister." He smiled and winked at his friend, then linked his arm with Avram's and guided him away, looking one last time as light died in heaven.

IV.

THE WOMAN IN white exited the metro bus that stopped near the cheder, and walked in semi-darkness to the old building. The few lights that still burned behind windows did not dispel the sense of isolation that subtly troubled Rebecca as she slowly made her way up the steps and through the door. Three young students quietly passed her by, and Rebecca felt as though they were observing her without actually looking at her. She realized that a woman was a rare thing in this place, especially a young woman whose luxurious dark hair was worn to her shoulders. She was unmarried, sans ring and wig. Sudden panic seized her brain, filling her with a sense of dread; for she felt suddenly like a creature that had wandered into a domain in which she was unwanted, unwelcome. But then Avram entered into the hallway, and his puzzled smile calmed her a little.

"I was looking for Samuel. Is he still here, do you know?"

"I saw him in the library earlier. Is something wrong?"

Rebecca shrugged, and then looked around to make certain no one was within hearing. "I'm a little worried. He didn't come home last night, and now it's getting late and . . ."

She suddenly felt a teardrop spill from her eye, and she tried to smile as she brushed it with a shaky hand. "I'm being foolish, perhaps . . ."

"No, Samuel's been acting — strangely. I saw that you were worried that night he unexpectedly brought me to your home for that amazing dinner. Come with me, and we'll find him." She followed and he led the way up the stairs and to the library, where indeed they found the reclining form of her brother, his slumbering head resting in folded arms that were surrounded by books

and sheets of paper. Avram bowed to her and exited the room. Timidly, the young woman approached the table and picked up one of the books, a slight book of Jewish mysticism. She scanned the other books, all of which were of like matter. Taking up a sheet of paper, she frowned at the bewildering characters that had been scribbled upon it. When her brother began to stir, she softly called Samuel's name. He raised a very pale face and gazed at her with eyes that were dark and confused.

"What are you doing here?"

"No," she said, holding before him a scolding finger. "What are you doing here? I've been worried sick."

"Just like a woman . . ."

"No," she firmly replied. "What, I shouldn't be worried when you are acting all crazy? This is not like you, Samuel. And what is all of this? You're suddenly obsessed with Kabbalah? Since when? You know the warnings of the Rabbis, how this stuff gets into you and takes hold of your brain. What, suddenly you're Isaac the Blind?"

Her brother's fist suddenly slammed onto the table. "Sha!" he shouted. "I don't need to be lectured. Who's with Mother?"

"Sadie Kline. Samuel . . ."

"No. I have studying to do. This is my profession. I am a teacher. Teaching requires study. Stop acting crazy and go home."

"I'm not the crazy one. When have you eaten last?"

"Food, is that all you think about?" He was glaring into his sister's eyes, and something in her inexplicable expression suddenly softened his heart. He noticed two figures hovering in the hallway near the library door. "Avram, are you driving Rav Sheldon home? May Rebecca accompany you? It's not a problem?"

"It's not a problem," Avram replied. And then, after a moment's hesitation, he added, "What about you?"

"I'll be here a while longer. I've got my bike." He smiled at Rebecca's worried face.

"We have a kitchen full of food. I've had a sandwich. I'm fine. Now, go home. Have you two eaten?" he asked the men. "Is any of that excellent soup left from the other night, Rebecca? Such good soup, my sister is a genius with food. Feed these hungry young men, Rebecca. I'll be home in a few hours. I'm solving a Torah puzzle that won't let go of my brain. Nu, it's what we do. Goodbye. Drive carefully, Avram, I only have one sister." Gently, he reached for her hand and brought it to his lips. His kiss was a tender thing.

Trying to smile, she turned to the other teachers. "Come, gentlemen." She gazed one last time at her brother. "And if you aren't home in a few hours, I'll be back."

He raised a reassuring hand. "I'll be home, already. Oy, women."

His sister forced a smile, then turned and led her companions from the room. Deeply sighing, Samuel stretched, then brought a sheet of paper forward and studied the symbols that he had scribbled thereon. No, the images were not correct. The symbol eluded him still. Once more he shut his eyes, for it seemed that he could only see the thing in a dream. Perhaps he could enter into a half-dreaming state of mind, and therein see the esoteric symbol that so beguiled, so haunted him.

What he sensed was another presence entering the room. Half opening his eyes, he saw the small form of the Rebbe studying titles on a shelf. A book was selected, and the old man turned to Samuel dark smiling eyes, eyes filled with wisdom, with concern. "Rav Samuel, you are still here." Samuel shrugged and tried to hide the sheets of paper before him with his arms. "So, still with this mystery? I hope that you aren't neglecting your duties to your students while you ponder this strange thing you are so concerned with. Remember why you are with us, Rav Samuel."

"Yes, Rebbe. I was just going over some old things, looking for a clue to my little mystery. It's a fascinating thing, you'll agree."

"Yes, fascinating; but important, no. And what will you do with your answer, should you find it? Write a book?"

"I like finding answers to questions, Rebbe. That's part of why I became a teacher, because in teaching my students I also teach myself."

"An excellent thing, education." The Rebbe reached under Samuel's arm and tugged on a sheet of paper that he finally pulled free. "Mysteries, of course, do not always illuminate, Rav Samuel. For some things, there are no earthly answers. This thing that has you so in its clutches, what do you think it is?"

"I can't say. That's part of the beguilement."

The Rebbe studied the diagrams that Samuel had scribbled with pencil onto the piece of paper he held. "We know that Hashem created all things with the holy alphabet, all things in all the worlds, the worlds of matter, the worlds of spirit. There is a legend of a secret name of G-d that is spoken only among the angels. This symbol that you imagine you have seen may be that awesome name, and like another name for G-d, is not to be uttered."

"Moshe spoke it."

"Did you actually here him speak it, or are you remembering a daydream? You're a dreamer, Rav Samuel, always with your head in the clouds. To be a dreamer does nothing to further our great work at this facility. We must be wide-awake if our program here is to succeed. My advice to you, my young friend, is to concentrate on your work as a facilitator. Don't be led astray by the secrets of Torah. Leave that to the tzaddik, who wears with wisdom the heavy ordeal of ultimate righteousness. Nu?"

Samuel smiled and nodded his head. "I'll do that, Rebbe. I promise not to let all of this," and he waved his arms over the books that covered the desk, "interfere with my work here."

"Good," the Rebbe told him, nodding sagely. "Now, clean up all of this and go home. You aren't looking well, and I am tired of worrying about you. Give me a break, please. Go home and eat a good meal. If I had a sister who had such a way with preparing meals . . . "

"I'll do that, Rebbe. I'll just finish here, and then I'll go."

The old man nodded, and then squinted his eyes as if trying to decide if he could believe what he had just heard. Nodding again, he turned and vacated the room.

Samuel yawned. He looked out a window, into darkness. Yes, he should go home. He would just go over this last book that he wanted to delve into, and then he would be gone. He opened the book and tried to read a passage, but the words were blurred. His heavy eyes lost their focus, and then shut.

V.

THE SMALL FIGURE entered the room, walked to the slumbering man, touched with a small hand one of the sheets of paper onto which symbols had been scribbled. He turned over one sheet of paper, picked up a pencil and placed it into his teacher's hand. Samuel stirred, uncertain where he was. He saw the delicate hand next to his own, the hand that gently took hold of his and began to guide it over the sheet of paper. Samuel watched with eyes that awakened, and saw the joined hands create a symbol with the pencil's point. He startled as that point suddenly broke. The symbol had not been completed. With trembling lips, he whispered Moshe's name. The boy leaned over him and patted his face with friendly fingers. A small white hand was placed onto the table, palm upward. Samuel deeply breathed as his hand that held the pencil was guided to Moshe's upturned palm. The splintered wood of the broken pencil was pressed into the innocent flesh. The facilitation continued, and a symbol was etched into flesh that parted and grew wet with blood.

The symbol was completed upon the palm. The boy touched his mouth to Samuel's ear and whispered the forbidden sound.

Samuel's body iced, and then violently shook. He was flung from his chair and fell heavily to his knees. He still held the boy's wounded hand, and gasped as that hand was pressed against his forehead. He wept, and tears mingled with the tiny streams of crimson that slide softly from the hand pressed against him. Through blood and tears he saw the others that had entered the room, those autistic kindred to Moshe, those children that had never looked directly at him. They did not look at him now as they quietly surrounded him, as they bowed as one in a circle of davening, praying. The room must have been unnaturally chilly, for streams of mist issued from the young mouths, those tender mouths that idiotically hung open. Samuel remembered and spoke a favorite psalm. "With the Word of G-d, the heavens were made, and with the Breath of His mouth, all their hosts." And he marveled at the sight before him, this circle of frail creatures than now appeared more angelic than human.

He turned to Moshe, to the eyes that, for the first and last time, looked directly into his own. There was a light behind those awesome eyes, and also a light behind the moving mouth, the mouth that sighed the magical letter's sound. Samuel kissed his hand and reached to press that hand against the boy's mouth. He felt the lips move beneath his hand as they uttered still the sacred name. He felt that angelic name gather in his flesh, and he shivered as it found his mouth. Swaying in time with those who encircled him, those who were now his kindred, Rav Samuel spoke the sacred name. ◉

W.M. Pugmire is a writer based in Seattle whose works tend towards the dark and unusual. He has had numerous stories published in various magazines and journals including *Deathrealm, Tales of Lovecraftian Horror* and *The Urbanite*. His latest collection, *The Fungal Stain and Other Dreams*, is available from Delirium Books. **M.K. Snyder** is a writer living in the Pacific Northwest.

Landscape, with Fish

BY KAREN HEULER

ILLUSTRATED BY WILL KOFFMAN

IN WHICH THE THEORY OF EVOLUTION SEEMS RELEVANT YET BESIDE THE POINT

"YOU GOTTA CONTROL your fish better," Willis said. "They're scaring my dog."

Tom nodded. "Didn't know they could go so far. It's interesting."

"The first time, yes," Willis agreed. "After that, it's nasty. The dog ain't the same."

"Easy now, it's just a fish."

"I hear they eat things you wouldn't think. I hear they slide right under doors."

"That ain't true, about the doors. You're thinking of mice, not fish. These fish eat mice, so they're more like cats. Only not so fast, I think. At least, I haven't seen 'em move that fast."

"I hear," Willis said slowly, "I hear they can get in the pipes. You know, you're sitting on the john . . . "

"Now that's damn foolish," Tom said. "That's maligning my fish."

"Keep 'em on a leash," Willis said flatly. "And put up some kind of fence."

"It's a good thing we're friendly," Tom said shortly. "Or I'd be annoyed." With that, Tom lowered his head and left. He came across one of those special-order fish of his on the well-worn path

back to his own house, and he kicked it a little. It made a kind of hissing sound.

"You watch it," he said to the fish. "You were meant to be eaten, you know." He looked at the fish, its big toothy mouth, its snaky head. "Though I wouldn't want to see you on my plate. Not without gravy anyway."

He poked the fish back to the pond and set to putting up a fence around it. "Fencing a pond," he grumbled. "Damn foreign fish."

He pounded in the posts and put up the mesh. The fish sort of hopped along the ground so it didn't have to be high. The job went easily.

He thought it was his imagination when he heard the pops against his window in the morning. He sat at the kitchen table and had his coffee first, that was his rule. He saw movements, like big flies, out of the side of his eyes, but he waited to catch them dead-on.

He saw one, finished his coffee, saw another, and got up.

They were leaving oval slimy smears on the windows and falling in the bushes around the house. A little stunned they were, obviously shook up till they got their wits about them again. It annoyed Tom when he saw them, because it meant there'd be trouble. He didn't have the kind of neighbors that would let a thing like this go by without comment.

He never actually saw them take off — he always caught them flying, instead — but he had to assume they did a kind of leap first, so he put up a higher fence.

That didn't stop them, and his windows were getting all smeared. Well, then, some kind of tent would do it. He stared at his little pond, which, when you started thinking about covering it, got a whole lot bigger. He sighed. It might be best if he got Willis to help him. It was hardly a secret he could keep.

Kind of strange he hadn't heard from Willis anyway, he thought, as he walked the old path to his neighbor's house. There were fish in the trees and they sometimes dropped on top of him with a wet thwack and an unpleasant snapping of teeth. They hadn't quite got the hang of it yet; they landed upside down and their teeth went nowhere.

Willis' place was looking a little off. The grass must have gone to seed because there was a whole flock of grackles standing off to the side making grackly cackles.

"Psst," Willis said, tapping on his window from inside. "Get in here."

Tom stepped inside.

"No problems getting through?" Willis whispered. "You didn't hear anything?"

Tom frowned. "Well, there's birds outside. I did hear that."

Willis drew in a long breath. "What were they saying?"

With that, Tom started to actually listen to the murmur outside, which wasn't exactly the regular kind of bird talk. He stepped to the window. The birds were walking around, meeting in groups. He listened hard.

The birds were saying, "WILLIS Willis Willis. WILLIS Willis Willis."

He stepped away from the window. "Now, that's creepy," he said.

Willis nodded. "Did they say anything about you?"

Tom listened again, but there was nothing but Willis in the air. "No," he said. "It's just you."

"What if they start lying?" Willis asked. "Won't nobody believe me over birds." His eyes got filmy. "How much do you think they know?"

Tom went out down the path and picked up a few of his fish. It seemed like they'd followed him part way. Some fish hopped along behind him back to Willis' place, and when he got to the grackles one fish reared up and grabbed a bird by the wing. Tom kicked it free, watching that bird rise up and join the others scattering overhead. As long as they were talking, they could talk about that.

Willis peeked from his window until the yard was clear and then he came out. "Those fish of yours," he said. "Mighty evil looking. They got a temper?"

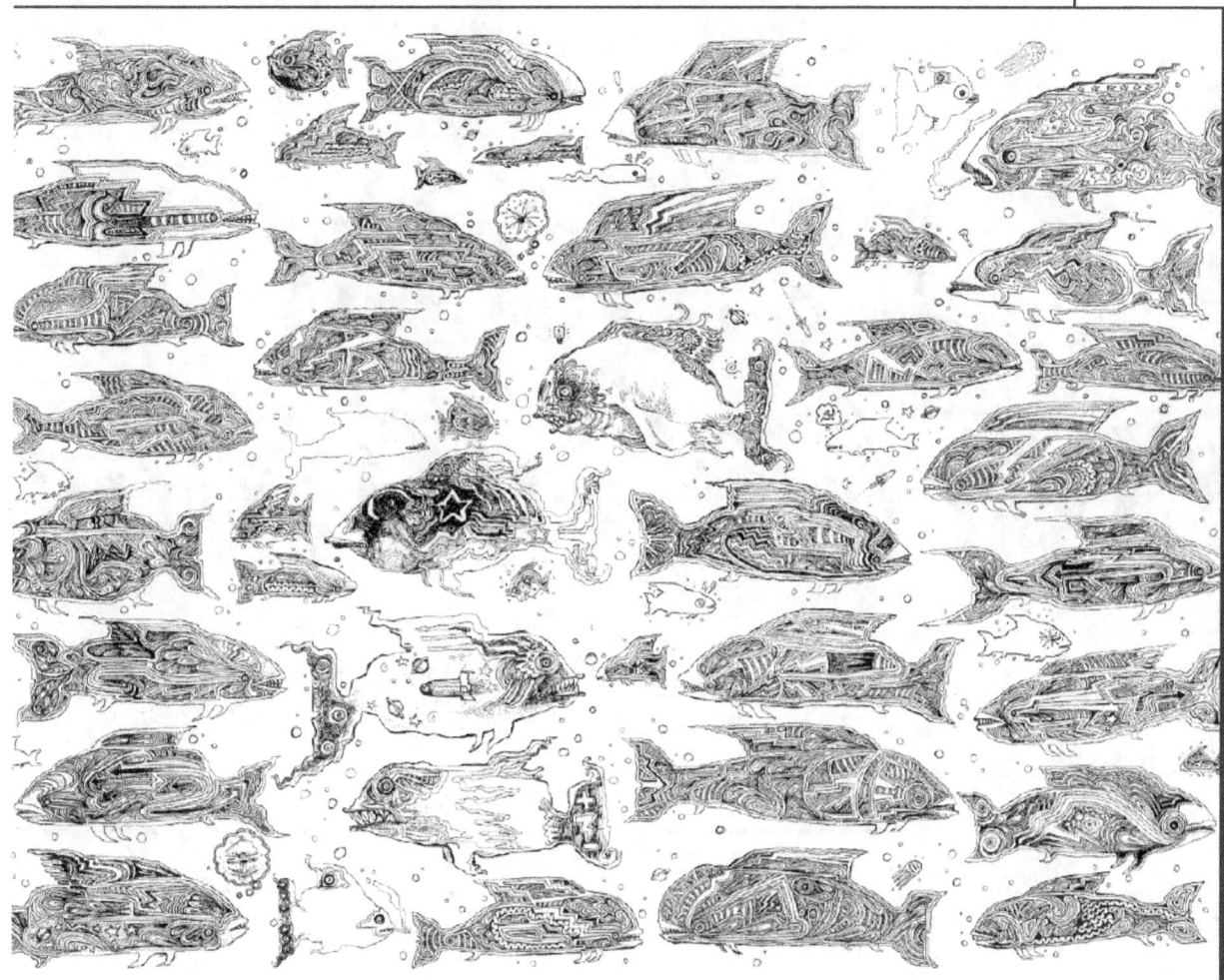

"Sweet as can be," Tom said. "They get attached, too, just like a dog."

"I think my dog ran out on me. Kind of miss him."

They stood for a while in silence, watching the fish. They were flapping on the ground, wiggling their tails back and forth till they started making a bunch of holes around the yard. Then they each settled into a hole and turned their heads towards the two men by the house.

"Well," Tom said. "Looks like they're planning on staying. You want 'em?"

Willis nodded. "I can see their attraction now. They'll keep the yard free anyway. And they're quiet — I like that."

Tom nodded. "Real quiet," he said. "You never hear them coming. You never know they're there."

Satisfied, the two men looked at the fish, and the fish in their trenches looked back at them. ☻

Karen Heuler's *stories have appeared in anthologies and in many literary and commercial magazines. She has published two novels and a short story collection, and has won an O. Henry award. Her latest novel, "Journey to Bom Goody," concerns strange doings in the Amazon. She lives, writes, and teaches in New York, which has its own share of strange doings.*

Events at Fort Plentitude

BY CAT RAMBO

ILLUSTRATED BY MARC ROBINSON

IN WHICH GOOD
MILITARY MEN
ARE ILL EQUIPPED
TO FACE MAGICAL
TEMPTATIONS

December 27th
Duke Theo's reign, 11th Year
Fort Plentitude

I N THE COLDEST nights of the winter, the fox women come out of the pine woods. Their flashes of hair are scarlet against the blue snow shadows. They sing an odd, whining song like puppies that have lost the teat.

Those are the nights that the sentries are changed every half hour, and they come back with cold-chapped lips and frost crystals along their jacket fronts. Every night by moonlight, we can see three or four of the animal women out among the snow banks. Ensign Caruso keeps track of the sightings in the fort's log book. Starting December 17th, there were five, immediately followed by two nights of solo visitations.

We post female soldiers more often on those cold nights, or married men with wives here in the fort. During last year in the trade village that preceded this fort, two men threw off their clothes and ran out into the snow chasing fox women. They found them frozen solid among the reeds of the river bank, the slender blades of ice impaling them. When their rescuers tried to disentangle them, the men shattered and were strewn across the ice. One-eyed Bill sent two of his wives down with whisk brooms to sweep the ice for fragments, but even so, the next summer, no one would eat frogs or turtles caught from that bank.

December 31st
Duke Theo's reign, 11th Year
Fort Plentitude

THE FOOD SITUATION continues to be dismal. If the Captain were a wiser man, he would seek to keep his troops busier. Instead they sit around the fort and vie to see who can complain the longest and hardest about the meals. It is impossible to spice them up, but we each carry a little skin of salt and pepper mixed according to our taste. The cook, it is rumored, has been using yellow salt to prepare our meals, chipped from a deer lick near the fort, and saving the finer salt to sell to the soldiers.

Jan 2nd
Duke Theo's reign, 12th Year
Fort Plentitude

CAPTAIN MERCER AND the cook have been arguing again. It is clear that the cook has been skimming off profits and that the paucity of our meals is due to his graft. Nonetheless, he makes meals for Captain Mercer and our officer's mess that are better than the average run, and so his corruption is tolerated. But as his supply of seasonings has dwindled, the Captain's temper has grown harsher.

I went so far yesterday as to break one of my three demon gems and send the beast to the southern Isles for an armload of fruit.

If the Sorcerer Corps knew, they would court-martial me for wasting such a valuable thing, but I couldn't help it. The hunger ate at me.

I told the demon to bring as much as it could carry, but it purposely made its arms as small as possible and brought me only three apples and a shriveled fig. I had meant to share my bounty with the soldiers. But when I saw the portion's scantiness I took it all for my own and ate it in one sitting, greedily, licking my fingers, devouring even the stems and seeds, and refusing to think about what I had done.

The demon stood staring at me all the time that I ate. It was a leathery-winged De-monica falciformus, with silky-tendriled hair and small black eyes that seemed intelligent.

Plinot argues that demons possess the equivalent intelligence of great Barbary apes or chimera, but this one seemed possessed of a peculiar, innocent malignity. It would have torn the flesh from my bones and rejoiced in it with a happy savagery.

Once I would have been angered by its mistake, lashed it with fiery words. But I have lost that energy — it ebbed away while I was worrying about food and cold.

At night I turn restlessly in my bed and send tiny sparks among my bedclothes to seek out the fleas and lice nesting there. The linens smell of smoke but this is better by far than bedbugs.

Even so, I cannot sleep. I am morose and at times cannot stop crying. I did not weep when they died, but now I cannot escape the tears, the visions of my dead.

Jan 28th
Duke Theo's reign, 12th Year
Fort Plentitude

THE DAYS AND nights are tedious. I tried to organize a party to go dig along the banks for cat tail roots, which according to a manuscript I read last week, are edible, indeed a

delicacy among some tribes. But the water had frozen so solid that there was no cracking it. We tried building fires atop the ice, but they sank, icy mud extinguishing them. We returned with nothing for our efforts — not even a brace of squirrels, because the soldiers were too loud and frightened every animal away.

The Captain has eighty troopers altogether, two Lieutenants, four sergeants, a cook, and myself, the only sorcerer in the group. All of us are miserable. Many of the men have come here in search of land grants for diligent labor, only to find a Captain ready to swindle them out of their holdings in exchange for stakes in dubious gold mines or counterfeit artifacts. Others like myself are one form of exile or another, trying to escape memories or pursuers. We are not in search of anything -- we know there is only cold and misery here for us in civilization's hinterlands.

February 2nd
Duke Theo's reign, 12th Year
Fort Plentitude

I LAY AWAKE last night belaboring myself with guilt for not saving the fruit for the nursing women here. I was greedy and foolish. Still, I cannot help but think that divided among the six of them, it would have been only enough of a taste to torment. My ministry to their health is surely worth this small price, to keep me lively and able to tend to their needs while they are caring for their babies.

I have talked the Captain into having Ensign Caruso cut up the old boiler and stove that we had sitting out near the dock. He uses the forge and cuts the metal into inch wide squares that the natives prize for making spearheads or hide scrapers. They trade us five gallons of dried corn for each square. The cook soaks it and makes it into porridge that the women eat. We must keep the babies healthy and strong.

In the spring a boat will come by and take the latest crop of babies back to the more settled lands, where people are cutting down trees and plowing fields and doing things that require healthy young workers, a new generation of settlers that can produce more in turn to man the forts and breed more babies. A cynical man might think it all part of the Duke's plan for expansion.

By the time the boat reaches Tabat, there will be half a dozen wet nurses aboard it, and the infants they supply, plus a small goat herd, sails full of just washed linens, and a few guards.

It has been a long and tedious winter. Their ranks will grow before spring comes, I am sure, since two additional women are pregnant. I see them fed better than most as well. The fort is too small to rate a doctor, so my dabbling in medicine suffices for the ailments here: dysentery, syphilis, boils, chilblains and pregnancies.

I have been thinking about the spring, and the fish markets of Tabat, and what my mother would cook: baked black bass, spiced eels, fried smelts, boiled mackerel, fried skate wing, codfish balls, baked trout, flounder cooked with bitter greens.

February 28th
Duke Theo's reign, 12th Year
Fort Plentitude

TODAY ENSIGN CARUSO brought me up to the gun tower. The wind whistled and screamed in my ears. We looked out across the river's white sweep, nearly a mile wide, and saw a dark mass moving across it, hesitantly at first, then with mounting confidence and speed. It came closer and we realized it was a herd of buffalo.

The ice was frozen thick enough all the way across that the animals, hundreds of them, could make their way to our eastern shore in fruitless search of fodder. The Captain dispatched several men to shoot strag-

glers in order to relieve the tedium of our meals. They killed several dozen and dragged them into the main yard of the fort.

I took my spyglass and watched from atop the outer wall. One-eyed Bill Lafitte and his wives moved back and forth on the scarlet ice, engaged in the same task of butchery. I imagined the ice under them, thick as layers of rock, shadows swimming underneath, deep down in the dark water.

Two wives stripped the hides off the carcasses and piled them on a rickety sled that the four other wives pulled. One of them had an infant tied to her back. I imagined the last wife was at home, tending the brood of children.

The human women were flat-faced and expressionless as they moved back and forth, taking the best of the meat to pile on the sled. The two Snake women were equally expressionless, but their tongues flickered in their reptilian faces, bright as flames against the winter white of their scales.

The cook roasted buffalo steaks and the fort smelled wonderful for an evening. Everyone went around smiling. But at table the meat proved stringy and tough. This far into winter, the animals are themselves half-dead of hunger and have little flesh to spare.

March 1st
Duke Theo's reign, 12th Year
Fort Plentitude

BIG WHITE, THE Shoshal shaman, came to see me. It was his third visit to my cabin, but the careful attention he gave every detail was the same as the first two times. I drew the structure of the universe and its concentric circles of realms, like a vast onion, on the wall and we debated its shape, for he insists that it is different, and that spikes from other realms protrude upon our own.

At least that is what I believe he tried to sketch out for me. His English is bad,

and my Shoshal non-existent. Rumor back at the College of Mages in Tabat held that the native mages, as well as the Snake people, are sophisticated in their understanding of magic, but this seemed like rank gibberish to me.

He made tea for both of us, a pleasant brew of flower petals and leaf fragments that made the inside of my cabin smell like summer. Tension dropped away as though I had shrugged it off with my buffalo-hide robe and hung it on the peg just inside the door.

He said, "Cold winter," and touched the demon gems on my desk, shaking his head sorrowfully. They do not believe in trafficking with spirits, and if he knew I had traveled here in one's arms, he might not speak with me again.

I asked Big White about the fox women, but he pretended not to know what I meant. I will have one of Lafitte's wives teach me more Shoshal, so I have words for the magical concepts I want to convey. If there is an easy way to drive them off, I would like to know.

March 2nd
Duke Theo's reign, 12th Year
Fort Plentitude

SLEPT EXCEEDINGLY WELL last night. The soldiers reported few fox women — perhaps Big White's presence keeps them at bay?

March 5th
Duke Theo's reign, 12th Year
Fort Plentitude

MY SISTER SARAH'S birthday. I sent her a pile of pelts last fall, martin and beaver, to make herself a coat, and warned her that, come winter, communications would be at a standstill due to the frozen river. I imagine her sitting in her comfortable, well-appointed house, eating sandwiches spread with a layer of butter and cress, the thin leaves from the greenhouse sharp and bitter against the bland bread.

She did not want me to leave Tabat, but after the failed experiment that killed Melissa and our unborn, I could not stay. Could not endure the eyes of the other mages knowing what I had done, how badly I had predicted events. Even this privation is better than that shame and sorrow.

I caught a handful of snow sprites in the afternoon, near the outer wall of the fort. They look like crane flies — insects as big around as a Spanish doubloon, but all wing and legs, and little else. They have tiny faces made of ice, but they do not speak. Why has God made these creatures that resemble us in all but intelligence?

Deep in the woods, Lafitte claims to have seen winter sprites as big as wolves or buffalo, enormous flying things that move along the edges of snowstorms, riding the winds in a flurry of icy chitin. I put the ones I caught in a glass jar. They fluttered for twenty-two minutes before succumbing to the heat of the room and dying, melting away into a noisome, clotted liquid that smelled of vinegar.

March 6th
Duke Theo's reign, 12th Year
Fort Plentitude

WHEN BIG WHITE came today, he shook his head and said over and over, bad, very bad. He led me outside the fortress walls and showed me ice runes on the outer walls, twelve feet high, two-thirds the height of the walls.

I asked him who had put them there, for I did not recognize the language or the writing, but it was clearly set there by sorcery. I had sensed none the night before, but I am so exhausted and hungry in the evenings that I do little but imagine meals at my mother's house back in Tabat.

He said winter and then a word I did not know, and indicated this entity had put them there. He threw handfuls of snow at the markings until they were partly obscured, but his face was troubled.

Inside the fort, I showed him a sketch Caruso had made of one of the fox women the night before. Did this woman draw the marks, I asked.

He shook his head and said dead, very bad, tapping the paper. That was all I could get out of him.

I asked him about trade for food, although I hated to throw myself on his mercy like that. But the pieces of iron were all gone and we have very few other goods. I indicated my belongings, trying to keep the whine out of my tone — surely there must be some equipment there he would like, I said. It would be easy enough to replace next year when spring came and the river thawed. Perhaps I'd even make the trip myself, and go to see Sarah in her fine new coat.

He took three small prisms, the most valuable objects there, and that evening dropped off two bushels of smoked trout. He must have said something to Lafitte as well, for one of the wives brought a sack of flour and another of dried meat. I distributed it among the pregnant women, despite the grumbling of the others, but saved a handful of each for myself.

March 7th
Duke Theo's reign, 12th Year
Fort Plentitude

LAST NIGHT I stayed awake, resolved to see the fox women. I sat in the tower with the sentry, watching the wood's edge. When I saw a blur of silver and blue fog, I looked with my spyglass.

She had Melissa's face and she looked straight at me.

It was only the bowl in her hand, steaming beef stew with dumplings, I knew, that kept me from running to her. The smiling

lure was too broadly painted and I realized it must be reading my thoughts somehow. No wonder men have run out to them.

In the morning, I told the Captain what I had discovered, that the fox women were trying to lure us out, but he would not listen. He had maps spread out across his desk. Come spring, he would take a patrol gold-panning, he said cheerfully to me. Wouldn't that be an adventure? His fingers trembled as he traced a line across the mountain, translucent blue as frost.

I broke my second demon gem and sent a letter to Tabat, to the Army Corps Headquarters. I explained our circumstances and the dangers. I explained that the Captain was unresponsive and possibly mad. I said 'Send food and more demon gems, and word of hope, or we will perish.' The demon took the scroll away. This one was feathered like a peacock, and had an odd snout that lolled loosely when it sniffed at me. I wait for the reply.

March 8th
Duke Theo's reign, 12th Year
Fort Plentitude

I HAVE BEEN advised that the winter has affected all frontier forts adversely and that food has been dispatched overland. Due to the frozen river, it will not reach here for at least six weeks. They sent no gems or other devices of aid. I have been officially demoted for using the gem, and reminded of their cost and scarcity.

In six weeks we will be licking the bones of the three horses left to us.

I sent to Big White to ask for more food, but he did not come. At length I donned snowshoes and walked over to the Shoshal camp.

Winter has not hit them as hard as it has us. There are fewer of them, and they spent the summer gathering food while we were building the fort walls. He gave me handfuls of smoked meat and a kind of thick biscuit baked with dried berries. I ate greedily until my stomach hurt and washed it down with gulps of hot bark-scented tea.

He said danger to the fort, babies, babies.

There is danger to the children, I asked.

He shook his head and drew a figure in the snow, a woman amid pine trees. You say fox women, he said, because hair red like fox. But not fox, not women. Babies that die go into the winter and make more. They want.

I was not sure what he was saying. That babies died and became fox women?

He tapped the figure with a gnarled finger. Baby want, he said. Just want want want. No more.

Was there no way to ward them off?

He shook his head. No.

March 9th
Duke Theo's reign, 12th Year
Fort Plentitude

YIELDING TO MY entreaties, the Captain sent several soldiers out hunting again, but they came back with only a bony elk, barely a mouthful or two of meat apiece. The cook stewed the heart for the officer's mess, but there was nothing but meat and water. The vegetables had gone long ago.

I found tracks all along the walls. Light tracks. Barefoot tracks, each foot tiny and arched, like that of a child. Snow sprites clustered motionless along the runes like a fuzz of white velvet.

I brought the Captain out to look at them, but he only smiled and patted my arm. This is a land of plenty, he said. In the summer, the bees will sing in the sour gum trees and drip honey into our mouths.

Another seven soldiers have died of dysentery so far this week, bringing our numbers to forty-two. We cannot make it till spring.

I lie awake trying to figure out a plan. Should I use my last demon gem and summon a final messenger to plead our case? Did they not understand that we will die without immediate surcease?

There are eight babies here now, aged between two and six months. They are thin and sickly, and they cry from the cold. I imagine the fox women taking them away, making them into new monsters. I imagine them walking across the snow slopes, clothed in glittering snow sprites, legs lengthening with each stride, faces elongating, hair falling into blazes of crimson longing.

Why do they only prey on the men? Are we weaker in our hearts?

March 10th
Duke Theo's reign, 12th Year
Fort Plentitude

FOR DINNER WE had watery gruel, a scant cupful per person, measured most strictly. More hunting parties dispatched.

March 12th
Duke Theo's reign, 12th Year
Fort Plentitude

LAFITTE AND HIS wives are dead. They found them frozen in their building. The children were all taken. We brought the last of their food to the fort, but it is sufficient for only a few more days.

Hunting parties still unsuccessful. We ate the last horse today.

March 13th
Duke Theo's reign, 12th Year
Fort Plentitude

THERE ARE MANY more of them now.

March 18th
Duke Theo's reign, 12th Year
Fort Plentitude

FINALLY I TAKE up the last demon gem. I walk across the fort, pass by the dead and dying. The cook is dead now, died of bloody flux, and the Captain has holed himself up in his office, crouched over his maps.

Faithful Caruso helps me. We sew an immense bag of buffalo hide, lined with the softest, warmest furs we can find among Lafitte's bales. We make it open at the top. We put the babies in it, one by one. The mothers that are still alive help us. I shatter my last gem and give the directions to the demon.

We can only hope a few will survive. The ones towards the outside of the bag will succumb to the cold first. They say freezing is not an unpleasant death. And when the demon arrives, perhaps it will only be delivering a package of frozen or drowned corpses. Demons are unreliable, to say the least.

But perhaps one or two will survive.

We watch the bag float up towards the sky. The demon is a kind I've never seen before, with rounded ivory horns and glittering silvery skin, immense wings that claw upward at the chilly air. It is quite splendid in its own way.

When night comes, I can hear the runes working on the outside of the walls, cracking them with icy pressures. Caruso and I wait in the watch tower, near the swivel-mounted cannon, snow sprites swirling around its barrel.

I can hear them whimpering with want, with longing, as they walk forward through the snow. When they finally come to claim us, will mine look like Melissa again? ℮

Cat Rambo *lives in the Pacific Northwest with her charming spouse, Wayne. She is a graduate of Clarion West and the Johns Hopkins Writing Seminars. Among the places in which her work has appeared are* Fantasy Magazine, Subterranean, *and* Strange Horizons. *It is indeed her real name.*

The Stone & Bone Boy

BY CALVIN MILLS

ILLUSTRATED BY SAM HEIMER

IN WHICH THE
FLESH AND THE
SPIRIT SADLY
BECOME ALL TOO
CONFUSED

INITIALLY, WHEN AUGUSTINE Ramos Martinez was born, his mother noticed nothing incredible about him. Nothing other than his being her very own, which was a blessing in itself because he hadn't come until seventeen years after her marriage. Later there did develop, in him, something that could perhaps loosely be described as a trait, but a trait that was repeated nowhere else in the Martinez or Ramos gene pools, nor in any other, at least as far as she knew.

Maria Pilar Martinez de Ramos was born and had been raised not far from the house in Segovia where she now lived. Her parents had passed away within six months of each other thirteen years after she was married. As a housewife, she was generally happy, except for her occasional bouts of boredom and loneliness. But now with a baby, she knew she would always have the child's attention and she believed the responsibility would be a welcome change.

Tomas Ramos, the boy's father, had gone bald at an early age. It seemed to be a symptom of his commanding a greater percentage of his brain than did the average accountant. He was a man of numbers and of details. Known in his office as the wizard accountant, he maintained a substantial position in the best firm in Segovia. Tomas Ramos was the person the other accountants came to when there was a problem with the books. In fact, he was such a magic worker with numbers that he created a schedule based on the Chinese calendar and on the rotation of the moon, which after long years of failure at the average haphazard way of going about it, enabled he and his wife to intermingle DNA.

This first and only child in the Ramos-Martinez family would be under serious threat of being spoiled between his doting mother and his prosperous father. It was a point of concern between the two to such an extent that each begged the other, long before Augustine was born, not to ruin the boy. They had no way of knowing he would live a different sort of life than most, and that their attentions would not therefore be of the utmost importance in the end.

THE FIRST INDICATION that something was amiss occurred when the boy was only fourteen days old. He became particularly fussy one morning and not long after Tomas arrived at work Maria telephoned, "I don't know what to do. His face is so red and he won't stop crying," she moaned, agitated, her voice stringing the words together in what was for her, an unusually high tone. This was all Tomas needed to hear. He dialed the doctor, then Maria again, to let her know the physician was on the way.

When Dr. Juarez arrived at the house, a thorough check was made of young Augustine. Nothing out of the ordinary was discovered initially. Doctor Juarez was a very polite, very expensive doctor who made house calls. He wore strong cologne and a gray suit. "When did he start all this?" he asked politely, though Mrs. Martinez de Ramos suspected a hint of feigned concern.

"This morning after his feeding," she replied.

"It's odd. Do you have a pacifier?" the doctor asked, shaking his head.

"I do," she said.

In a moment the pacifier was in the doctor's hand and then it was in the baby's mouth. When the boy took it he grimaced then screamed much louder than he had before.

"Let me look at his mouth," the doctor said. He pulled out a small mirror and a tongue depressor. Maria pulled the pacifier away again.

"Well, isn't that strange?" he mumbled, peering inside.

"What is it?" Maria asked quickly.

Doctor Juarez didn't answer. Instead he shuffled around in his bag, brought out a pair of tweezers, wiped them with an alcohol pad and wrinkled his face with concentration. He worked at something in the child's mouth.

"There we go," he said. He pulled the tweezers up to eye level between himself and Maria to reveal a shard of bone, opaque and narrow but sharp on both ends. Augustine settled down almost immediately. Opening and closing his mouth, spittle came in strands between his gums. Then without the noise of his crying it was quiet in the room. Mrs. Martinez de Ramos relaxed, feeling the air around her suddenly tangible again as the adrenaline slowed and her numbness seeped away. The baby gasped to take regular breaths, the crimson in his face fading.

"What is it?" Maria gasped.

"It appears to be a bone shard," the doctor said, as if he didn't quite believe it.

"But he doesn't eat meat," she blurted. She looked as if someone had suggested there were only eleven Stations of the Cross. The doctor laughed quietly. "No of course he doesn't, but this isn't a bone from meat, it's a bone from him."

"How do you mean?" Maria asked, her face blank. Her eyes were wide and staring as if she were trying to read lips.

"Well it's hard to say exactly why, but there seems to have been a bone chip in the

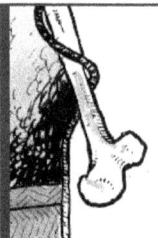

child's gums and it has worked its way out."

"When I had my wisdom teeth pulled that happened to me," Mrs. Martinez de Ramos said. "They had to break the teeth to get them out. The slivers came out very slowly, some of them weeks after the teeth were pulled."

"Exactly," he encouraged. Then he looked again at the shard and said, "Strange though, that he would have any loose bone floating around. I only looked to his mouth because he was acting like he was teething, though you know it's much too soon for that."

"I'm glad it was only that," Maria said as she retrieved Augustine from the crib. "He seems much better now." She pulled him to her abruptly as a mother does with a child after any scare, allowing the spit on his chin to darken her silk shirt. She inhaled his slightly sour smell and found it comforting.

When the doctor left, Maria offered the child her breast and he took it happily. After he fed she telephoned Tomas and relayed the news to which he responded only, "I don't understand it."

"Neither do I," she said. "But everything's fine now."

ONE MONTH LATER, it seemed to be Maria's overactive imagination when she first gathered that the boy's overall expression had changed. She held him sitting up, perched on her knees with his feet in her lap. She was sure it was an ill-perceived observation, but he seemed to be distracted, as if something had been troubling him. Maria went about her business and tried not to think about it. Two, then three days passed, and still she could not shake her intuition that something was annoying the boy.

On the fourth day when she had finally settled her nerves and convinced herself that everything was fine, Augustine leaned forward, sneezed violently and spit out a small red stone. "Ay Dios mío," she said, more to herself than to him. "Where did that come from?" She picked up the stone from the blanket on which he was sitting and squeezed it between her fingers, then be-

tween her fingernails, hoping that it was only some soft bit of fluff from the carpet, but it was not. She looked wide-eyed at Augustine, who, for the first time in four days, seemed pleased. The stone was only the size of a pea but it was as rough and sharp as volcanic rock. She picked up the telephone and dialed Doctor Juarez directly.

"Yes, it's like a rock," she said.

"No," she said, "I don't think he got it off the ground and put it in his mouth then sneezed it out. I think it came from inside him."

"Well I suppose it's possible," she said after a lengthy pause.

"Okay. I'll try not to worry," she said, then inhaled slowly. "But Doctor Juarez, his expression has changed."

"Okay," she said, "yes, I'll call you," and she hung up the phone.

Maria walked to the kitchen staring at the small stone between her fingertips. She squeezed it once again to feel the sharp edges. She started to drop it into the garbage but couldn't let go of the thing. Instead she opened the cupboard where there were jars of baby food in neat rows. She took down a jar of split peas, dumped the contents down the sink, rinsed and dried the jar then put the small red stone inside. She carried the jar around much of the afternoon, looking at it every so often. Finally, just before Tomas would arrive home, she put the jar in the utility drawer in the kitchen. She decided she would pretend it hadn't happened.

SIX MONTHS LATER the items in the jar in the utility drawer downstairs numbered twenty-nine. There were sixteen bone shards and thirteen stones.

Upstairs in their bedroom, after the baby had gone to sleep Maria pleaded, "You have to tell me if you've ever dropped him." There were tears in her gray eyes.

"Please don't start with that again. I've told you no. I've never dropped him," Tomas moaned. He undid his bow tie with a series of exaggerated movements tossing it onto the bed.

"But you can tell me. I just have to know why he has so many bone shards floating around in him. It could have been some major trauma that we somehow overlooked. The doctor said maybe if he had broken several bones."

"He hasn't broken several bones!" Tomas shouted. "How could we fail to notice several broken bones?" He threw his jacket and vest to the floor then turned on her in anger taking her by the collar of her robe. Her hair was still not brushed from that morning. He brought her face close to his. "What about you?" he shouted. "Did you drop him? Did you fall while you were pregnant? Maybe this trauma occurred when he was still in the womb!" He let go of her then, pushing her away from him slightly. Tomas nodded his head repeatedly, his eyes ardent, fixed on hers.

"Oh no," she cried out, astonished. Her face seemed to be melting. "You can't think I did any of this," she screeched. Suddenly she caught herself. She looked strangely but purposefully at an empty section of wall and put her hand over her mouth. Her face smoothed over. On the other side of that particular wall was the nursery. She began to whisper, "No, no, you can't." Her face twisted up again and tears rolled down her cheeks and along each side of her nose. Her eyes searched his desperately.

Tomas only stared at her silently for a moment.

"You can't think — " she began quietly.

"No," he interrupted in a limp voice. "I don't think that."

Tomas Ramos dropped his head. "You just have to understand how it feels to be accused of something like that. I can't take that again and again," his words grew quiet. His anger faded.

She observed his face closely. Hers was still panic-stricken.

Tomas' breathing was heavy, his head tilting back as he drew breath in and forward when he exhaled. "I didn't drop him. Nobody did anything. Please don't ask me again. You know how much I care about our son. You're not the only one who's concerned."

Maria came to Tomas then and threw herself against him. He held her in his arms. She was sobbing. He clenched his jaw, pretending that he was much stronger than she was.

"I'm sorry," she said.

"Anyway, while Doctor Juarez is so busy speculating about imaginary traumas, what about the stones? What does he say about that?"

"He doesn't know," she said. "He says there is no explanation."

"Exactly. So maybe there is no explanation for any of this," Tomas said.

The two held each other close while Tomas directed them, taking tiny shuffling steps toward the bed where they sat down slowly, then laid down together quietly until Maria announced, somewhat heartened, "Yes. Maybe it's just strange enough, not to need an explanation."

ALMOST ONE YEAR had passed since their confrontation in the bedroom and Maria had settled into her role as the mother of a toddler with a rare, innocuous gift. She became desensitized to the phenomenon simply by the frequency of the occurrences and by the overall health, growth, and good nature of the boy.

Doctor Juarez referred the case to an entire team of pediatric doctors in Madrid who did studies, especially of the stones. They found that these were similar to kidney stones in their shape and composition, and differed only in color and in the manner in which they were expelled. Some came from his nose, others from his throat and at least one from his ear. The doctors took stool samples searching for additional occurrences. Unfortunately for the doctors and their trouble, they found none there. They seemed to agree however that the boy was in no immediate danger.

When Maria brought Augustine to Madrid for his appointments, she made a habit of dressing herself and Augustine in their best clothes. She even bought the boy new clothes for his visits to the eager specialists. She enjoyed the trip to the capital and the attention given to both of them over the curious condition her son continued to display. She began to feel so important that she once turned down a proposed appointment time saying that she and Augustine already had an engagement, which they did not, and could the team please find another time in their schedules and call her back.

Downstairs in the kitchen, in the utility drawer there were only screwdrivers, twist ties for garbage sacks, and orphaned bolts and thumbtacks. The jar had made its way to the nursery. Not only had it been out where people might see it, but Mrs. Martinez de Ramos had scrapped off the label with a razorblade and decorated the jar lid with glue covered with silver and gold glitter. She was currently awaiting the delivery of a small glass showcase with built in-lights. The commission had gone to a hobby shop owner just down the street.

TWO WEEKS LATER the case arrived. It was a thing of beauty. Its bottom, top, and sides were all of purple heart, a fine rare wood from Africa, stained and covered with several coats of shellac. The glass shelves were free of even a single particle of glue or dust. The florescent lights, one hidden in the top and another in the base, illuminated the thick plate-glass shelves so that they beamed a faint blue-green. The now white bone shards glowed in the soft cool illumination as if under a black light. The couple spent the first evening with the case trying to decide how to display the pieces. They tried lining them up perfectly spaced and in order of size. They tried the stones and the bones on separate shelves. They ended up however, perhaps for sentimentality over the baby food jar, making small piles of the pieces all mixed together. They seemed much more weighty displayed in that manner.

Not long after the display case was delivered and installed in the posh living room between the Renoir replica and the small bronze bust of Mozart, someone, Maria sus-

pected the hobbyist, gave a detailed account of the story to the local press.

When contacted by the reporter, Maria was titillated but, fearing the effects of such media attention on Augustine and on their lives, she refused comment. However, she only did so after accidentally confirming that the story was true.

The article came out on a Thursday. Mr. Ramos was inundated with questions at work. He shook his head and acted very defensively at first but eventually had some open conversations only with the co-workers he most respected. Tomas Ramos' constitution was as stoic as it had always been, but he was forthright with the answers to their questions. When their curiosities were satisfied, Tomas was left alone to resume his work and he did so with some relief.

Mrs. Martinez de Ramos received two phone calls at home that day. She took Augustine in his carriage out to the newsstand and bought ten copies of the paper, though she was appalled by the headline pertaining to her son, The Stone and Bone Boy. The next day there were more calls and knocks at the front door, which Mrs. Martinez de Ramos left unanswered.

THE FOLLOWING DAY, the second day of the media blitz, Maria put on a nice dress and paid special attention to her hair and makeup. She dressed Augustine in his newest outfit, sat him in his highchair in the middle of the kitchen floor, and wrapped a towel around his neck.

Augustine was scheduled to have his haircut but Mrs. Martinez de Ramos had no intention of braving the small crowd on her front lawn without his appearance being at its best. There was another knock at the door just as she was approaching him with the scissors. She stopped where she stood, two steps from him, and listened carefully. Augustine quite happily made noises with his mouth, wiggled his fingers and kicked at the highchair with his heels. Mrs. Martinez de Ramos smiled and proceeded toward the boy nervously because she had not taken scissors

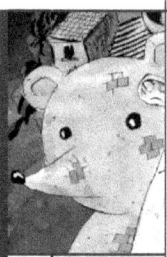

to anyone's hair since she was six years old when she ruined her own just before class pictures.

WHEN TOMAS ENTERED, his wife was sitting on the couch, her eyes puffy and the tip of her nose red. She held in one hand a handkerchief, with the other she balanced the boy on her lap. Augustine smiled at his father and raised his arms. His bangs were crooked and short. A tuft of hair curled over his ear.

"Hello," Tomas said, just as his wife noticed him standing there. "Is anything wrong?" he asked.

Maria answered sullenly, "Look what I've done."

"You cut his hair?" he asked, sighing, then smiled less than half-heartedly.

"Yes."

"Why?"

"I was supposed to take him out to get his haircut. But with all the cameras I couldn't take him out with his bangs in his eyes."

"So, you cut his hair so that you could take him out for a haircut?" he asked pensively.

"Yes. But when it turned out like it did I couldn't go out there," Maria sniffed. "Because of them." Mrs. Martinez de Ramos raised her hand flipping the handkerchief in the direction of the front door.

"They're not there Maria, they've gone," he said softly.

Mrs. Martinez de Ramos glared at her husband. She used two hands to hold onto Augustine until she was standing. Then she balanced him on her hip while she carefully peeled back the curtain next to the door. "They've gone already?" she asked, shaking.

"Yes."

"Why?"

"I don't know," he said, staring at her incredulously.

"I don't understand," she said, her voice unreasonably loud.

"Well, let's just be glad that — "

"Glad?" Maria shouted. She put Augustine down on the couch. The boy began to cry. She, seeming not to notice, rushed to the front door, flung it open and stepped onto the porch to look up and down the street. "It's not even dark yet," she said.

"What are you doing? How can you be angry; did you expect they would stay forever?"

Mrs. Martinez de Ramos shut the door slowly, while looking at the floor of the entryway. She turned the bolt in the lock and clicked off the porch light. Leaning against the door she began to weep.

"I don't understand," he said.

"You wouldn't understand," she said. "You just wouldn't."

TWO MONTHS LATER Tomas met his wife's gaze briefly as he opened his mouth, but his eyes darted off before he spoke. "I have to get to work," he said.

Tomas finished tucking in his shirt, zipped up his pants and fastened his belt. He took her by the shoulders briefly. "Please get up. Do something with your hair and get out of the house today." He kissed her forehead and grinned mechanically. "I'm off," he said.

When she heard the front door close Maria ran her hands through the mess of curled hair atop her head. She pulled at it, tried to press it down on one side, then sighed and slid her legs out of the bed so that her feet touched the cool floor. Augustine began to cry then. She walked slowly out the door of their room toward the nursery. Before she reached Augustine the telephone rang. She closed the door against the sound of Augustine's whaling and hurried to pick up the phone.

"Hello, yes this is Maria Pilar Martinez de Ramos," she said, trying to sound very personable.

"Oh, from the hospital," she said.

After she listened for a few seconds she asked, "And do you know when the doctors would like to reschedule?"

"Will they call me later and let me know then?"

"I see. And I don't suppose I could speak with any of them could I?"

"Yes, they're not there now, I understand."

"No, there's no message. Thank you."

Maria put the phone down slowly and stood in front of it for a moment. Augustine was still crying in the nursery. She turned slowly and moved to his room to comfort him. After a change of clothes she brought him to her where he fed only briefly, then refused her breast. He would prefer some solid food, she thought. After all, he had teeth of his own now.

With Augustine in arm Maria descended the staircase. She turned to walk through the front room to the kitchen but stopped when she saw the case. The cool, blue-green light glowed on the mantle. The room was otherwise dark with all the shades drawn. After absorbing the image she pulled back a curtain and peered out at the day. It was gray and cloudy. She touched the cold pane of glass with her nose. Maria imagined the clouds were purposefully dangled around her, perhaps caught on the roof of their house.

Augustine babbled when she walked toward the case. She touched the switch, ready to turn off the lights. She paused, a look of concentration creeping across her face.

TWO HOURS LATER Maria and Augustine, who were now bathed and dressed presentably, strolled down the cobblestone-street to the newsstand. This time she picked four different newspapers, the most respectable she could find. Back in the house she spread them out on the floor in the front room and skimmed through them. When she found an article she liked she tore it out and started a pile of clippings. She underlined the names of those reporters and wrote in the margin which newspaper they worked for. When Tomas came home for the mid-day meal Maria cleaned up the newspapers and clippings, hiding them under the cushions in the sofa. After his siesta when he left again for the office she threw away the papers, and with the clippings in hand, picked up the telephone.

* * *

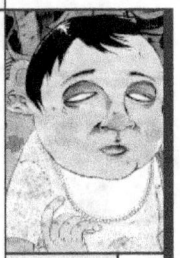

THE NEXT DAY Tomas was surprised when Maria woke with him. He came down the stairs to the smell of frying onions and potato. She added the eggs and cooked the omelet over a low flame while she made coffee. He ate his breakfast at the table while she rambled about the house. She came down, her hair tended and Augustine's long bangs wetted and combed back. She kissed Tomas goodbye and went out the door with the boy.

When she returned that evening Augustine's hair was cut and hers was trimmed and styled.

"IT'S SO GOOD to see you out and about," he said to her that night in bed.

"Thank you," she answered.

Tomas hoped she might say more but she seemed exhausted and only snuggled into the bed on her side, breathing deeply.

THE FOLLOWING DAY she helped Tomas out of the house and told him that some friends wanted to meet him for mid-day meal at their house across town. They would have a nice paella, she said. When Tomas reluctantly left, with a bottle of wine under his arm, Maria tidied the house. She dressed, then bathed and dressed Augustine and combed his hair.

"Maria Pilar?" the reporter asked when he came to the door.

"Yes, come in," she said. She waved her arm grandly and asked him to sit on the sofa across from the mantle. She had left the curtains drawn hoping he would notice the lighted case.

During the brief introductions he wrote some things in a notebook. When he finally eyed the case, he tilted his head sideways and asked, "Are those the pieces?"

"Yes, feel free to take a look," she encouraged. She rose when he did and smiled graciously. She seated Augustine on the floor on a blanket. The boy gurgled and chewed on his fingers. His dark eyes were wide, his forehead and cheeks smooth and pale under his dark bangs. She watched him happily for

a moment while the man looked inside the glass case.

"So these are the actual pieces?" he asked. He had emphasized the word actual. Maria, caught off guard by his tone, answered, "What do you mean?"

"I mean, these are the very stones and the bones that came from your boy?"

"Yes," she said, drawing the word out as if it had three syllables. She smiled then, still attempting to recover her composure.

"Hmm," he said, and looked into the case again, frowning this time.

"I'll give you the doctors' names."

"Yes, of course, I'd like to talk to the doctors. And you say they have actually witnessed the expulsion of some of these pieces?"

Maria closed her eyes then looked from side to side before staring at him. "No," she said, "Doctor Juarez found the first one, but the specialists on the team did not."

"I see," he said.

"I have been here for all of them except a few that I found in his crib in the mornings."

"So you are the only witness to any after the first one. Is that right?"

"No, my husband — " she started.

"Your husband, yes, but anyone else?"

Maria was quiet for a moment. She blinked and held the fingers of one hand with the other hand, gripping them tightly. She continued to smile through the remainder of the conversation, though it was not a genuine smile and it made her cheeks cramp.

Toward the end of the conversation he said, "You understand I will need to witness one of these expulsions. I will start on the story but it won't get approval from the editor until I talk to the doctors, and witness one expulsion. So what I need you to do is pay close attention. When you think it's going to happen let me know and I will come."

"Okay. That shouldn't be too much trouble," she answered. "It shouldn't be long now. He hasn't produced one for almost a week. It's usually not much longer than that."

When the reporter left he smiled vaguely and shook her hand. She realized then that he had hardly looked at the boy and hadn't spoken to him. He had paid him no attention whatsoever.

WHEN TOMAS RETURNED, he found his wife pleasant but distracted. She listened intently when he spoke about the lunch and about his day at work. She even let him make love to her twice after Augustine went to sleep. He was suspicious but happy and he let it go at that. The lovemaking after having missed his siesta made Tomas as tired as she was. They both soon fell into a sound sleep.

THREE DAYS LATER Maria was relieved to see that Augustine was a bit under the weather, thinking it meant he would likely be producing something soon. When Tomas left for work she called the reporter who came moments later in a cab. She sat Augustine on the floor on his blanket and offered the reporter a cup of tea.

Three hours later when Tomas was due for his mid-day meal Maria asked the reporter to leave and come back in three more hours. He was irritated and walked out with his head wagging from side to side, but he did as she asked.

When he returned there was still nothing and throughout the afternoon and early evening there was nothing. When she asked him to leave again when Tomas was due home the reporter said, "Please call me when you're sure."

"It's hard to say," she said. "It should be soon though."

"I hope so," he said. He put on a worn brown coat and went out the door.

"Thank you," she said after him as walked across the street.

THE FOLLOWING DAY Augustine seemed to be feeling better. Maria could do nothing but wait. That day she was a little more careless while dressing, and the day after, a little more. Five days later Tomas was upset with her again. When he left the house she called the reporter.

His voice was anxious for news. "No he's not showing any signs," she said.

"Well, he'll do something sooner or later won't he?" he asked.

"He always does," she answered, her voice quiet this time.

"Please call me when you suspect something," he said, breathing shortly, then he made an excuse to get off the line.

TEN DAYS LATER it was the reporter who called Maria. She broke into sobs upon recognizing his voice.

"I'm a bit concerned," he said.

"So am I," she moaned. "He hasn't passed anything in such a long time."

"Maybe he's cured," the man said smartly.

"He's not stopped before; why should he now?" she said. "Haven't you talked to the doctors?"

"Yes," he said plainly.

"Are you very sure you have to witness one? It's just that it's hard to say exactly when it will happen."

"Sorry, I'm afraid so," he said. "Call me if you know anything."

"All right," she said, and she hung up the phone. She looked at Augustine then. He was happily tearing the pages out of one of his books. She hadn't even noticed. The colorful pages lay spread out around him where he'd dropped them. He babbled and made a wide smile when his mother called his name.

SIX MONTHS LATER on the mantle in the front room, there was an empty space between the Renoir replica and the small bust of Mozart. The newspaperman had called a month before to tell Maria he was taking an assignment in the Middle East. It was just as well, she thought. She had told Tomas everything and he was not at all pleased. Tomas locked the case away in the broom closet by the back door and guarded the only key.

Maria could have opened the door had she cared to. But when Augustine failed to produce any further bits of bone or stone,

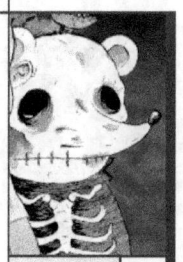

there was not much point. The doctors were still curious, if not devoted to the cause, but Maria stopped making the trips to Madrid.

"Tomas," she said, pensively one night, her eyes wide in their dark bedroom. "I have to know. You must forgive me for asking you."

"What is it," he asked, his tired voice something like an uneven breath.

She sat up in the bed then. Tomas saw that she was frightened by what she was about to say. When she began to sob he did not move to comfort her. "I have to know the truth Tomas. Didn't you ever drop him?"

Tomas didn't answer her. Suddenly he could not muster the energy to move at all or to say anything.

THE NEXT MORNING Maria slept late. Tomas had gone to work and she wondered when she saw that the clock read nearly eleven, why Augustine had not woken her with his crying. She got up and hurried to his crib where the boy lay, smiling, sound asleep. In the half-lit room she stared at him and his queer grin. He was so very still. It was not until she reached in to pick him up that she understood he was gone.

"WHEN YOU FOUND him, were any of his blankets over his mouth or was he lying face down?" Dr Juarez asked when he came out of the room.

Tomas looked at Maria. She shook her head.

"Then we can probably rule out suffocation. Did he have a fever or any infections that you know of?" he asked.

Maria shook her head again, not looking up.

"It looks a little like sudden infant death syndrome, but SIDS usually affects much younger children. Sometimes infants just stop breathing; it usually happens like this at night. We'll try to find you some answers. It's a dreadful thing for you, Maria and Tomas. I'm so very sorry." Dr. Juarez reached out to each of the parents who were sitting on the edge of their bed. Neither of

them took his hand. He placed an empty hand on Maria's shoulder and one on Tomas'.

Maria blurted out as if from sleep, "We need an autopsy."

Tomas pretended like he hadn't heard her.

Dr. Juarez said, "Yes, of course, that's what they do if the cause can not be immediately determined."

MARIA, TOMAS, AND Dr. Juarez accompanied the boy's body to the hospital. Dr. Juarez left the couple in a waiting room upstairs and took the body to the morgue in the basement alone. He spoke with the mortician and as a favor the man did the work while the parents waited with a priest upstairs.

When the mortician arrived upstairs his face was aghast. Not having known the man or because of their grief, the couple seemed not to notice his countenance. Only the priest and Dr. Juarez anxiously anticipated his words.

"Mr. Ramos, I have found the exact cause. I don't understand it. That is to say, I recognize the end but not the means. I have telephoned the specialists in Madrid and they will need to see the heart."

Dr. Juarez only stared at the man. Maria sat with her head in their hands. Tomas was sitting upright his hands on his knees. They were not touching each other.

"Your son's heart failed because of these." The man pulled a white paper envelope from his lab coat pocket. He opened the envelope and poured the contents into the palm of his hand. There were a dozen smallish shards of bone. "The arteries, the ventricles, they're full of these."

Maria screamed out. Tomas, instead of holding her, leaned away from her startled. Dr. Juarez looked at the mortician and shook his head from side to side. The priest approached Maria. The mortician then looked at Dr. Juarez apologetically as if he had not been tactful. The doctor reflected his gaze with a slight shrug as if to say, it's of no consequence.

* * *

TWO DAYS LATER Dr. Juarez came to speak with Maria and Tomas about the arrangements. He carried in his pocket a newspaper clipping, which he showed to the parents. He did not give it to them to read but explained to them that it was from the same tabloid paper that had published the first article, The Stone and Bone Boy. "They've got a hold of the fact that your son has passed away," he said.

Tomas, furious, glared at Maria, suspecting now that she had been at fault when the first one was published. Feeling as he did, as if he did not know his wife, he considered momentarily whether or not she might be responsible for this as well.

"I and the other doctors have some concerns about this that we're not quite sure if you have considered," the doctor said. "The team from Madrid has finished their study of the heart. They're sending it back today to be interned with the body. You said the gravesite is prepared?"

Tomas, opened his mouth, his eyes were narrow his fists clenched. "Yes," he said.

"I'm afraid, well, we are all afraid, that with the tabloids and all. You see, we're afraid of grave robbers. You understand; medical curiosities and all that. There are still museums in other parts of Europe that purchase these things."

Tomas and Maria both stared at the man. They sat very still.

"I don't suppose you would consider cremation?" Dr. Juarez lifted one eyebrow waiting for an answer.

"You know the Church doesn't allow it," Mr. Ramos said shaking his head in disbelief.

"Yes of course," he said. "I have just one other suggestion to make then. It's quite unorthodox but you see it's the boy's heart we're worried about here."

ONE MONTH LATER in the Martinez Ramos house, Maria sat at the kitchen table. It was a cold morning and she had a warm bowl of white rice in front of her. Tomas had been back to work for nearly three weeks now.

Maria could see the door of the closet under the stairs from the kitchen table. She looked back and forth between the door of the closet and the bowl of rice. There was one less thing to worry about now, she thought. The small organ had been cleaned, wrapped in gauze, and preserved in a medical specimen jar.

Maria decorated the jar with small crosses of glue, which she sprinkled with gold glitter. She and Tomas had emptied the closet, lined the walls with red velvet and placed in the center a small gilt table on which sat the case and the jar. Keeping it in the house seemed a morbid idea at first, even to Maria. Tomas had reminded her of the relics held within the walls of the Cathedral and that some of those were of flesh and bone. Dr. Juarez arranged for the priest to visit them and to anoint and bless the secret resting-place.

Tomas still refused her a copy of the key, only allowing her in when he was at home. However, it was less than a week after he'd gone back to work before Maria had learned to trip the lock with a kitchen knife.

Maria Pilar Martinez de Ramos looked again at the bowl of rice in front of her. She pushed her spoon into the center of the bowl and slid it across the table. She went to the drawer for the knife then to the closet. When Maria retrieved the jar she sat down again, staring at it for sometime before she pulled a scrap of paper from her pocket, picked up the telephone, and began to dial. ☻

Calvin Mills was raised behind the redwood curtain in Eureka, California. His stories and creative nonfiction essays have appeared in *Short Story, The Caribbean Writer, Tales from the South Vol. 1, Timber Creek Review, Southern Indiana Review,* and other journals and magazines. He currently teaches English at Peninsula College in Port Angeles, Washington — the last town Raymond Carver called home.

Renovations

BY MATTHEW PRIDHAM

ILLUSTRATED BY DANIELE SERRA

IN WHICH A VERY
HAUNTED HOUSE
STRIVES VALIANTLY
FOR REDEMPTION

We are lonely, so lonely.

We have been alone here with our sorrows for such a long time.

One hundred years have passed since last we spoke to a neighbor and then only to fight. Surprisingly, the nights have not been the most difficult times to endure. In the darkness, the world herself seems forlorn: insects chitter and chirp at their solitude, every leaf dragged to friendless fates by a wind blowing nowhere, the moon shines down on the unconscious. No, during the night we can pretend silence is the most natural state.

In the shadows we can even play at dreaming.

It is only when daylight first licks at our lawns, when our askew doors light up with merciless day, it is only then that the sadness overwhelms our pretensions of normalcy and we remember we are alone. No matter the strength of our dreams, they are as easily shattered by morning as our windows have been by rocks and bottles.

Sometimes we forget there are others, that beyond the row of gnarled trees that border our land there are those with whom we used to speak. We sense them even now in our isolation, strong and healthy and brimming with all sorts of life. There are new presences too, creatures such as us yet so young and vibrant they've hardly had time to awaken. Imagining their impudent and lazy ways brings us some of the only joys we experience anymore. These musings, though, soon lead to anguish, to bitterness.

We can only cherish whatever has been left of our body by the petty cruelties of time, examining with fading pride our sturdy stairs, a hallway spared of debris by fortuitous placement, perhaps a wardrobe here with a working door, maybe a couch there with fewer stains than it might have had. We can barely pretend that this solitude is a splendid one, that it has brought dignity to our frame, that the others could only wish for this degree of peace.

These fantasies, too, rot and crumble under the weight of our pain. We did not choose this desertion: we are shunned. When memories of us stir, fear chokes them back into intentional amnesia. The young whom we sense on every side of our borders whisper of us as diseased in titillated tones. The old, our friends from our own youth, the old pretend we burnt to cinders long ago and if they ever speak of us, it is with that sorrowful disdain one has for those who have brought about their own destruction. There was a time when we hoped for rejuvenation, when we cried to those friends and said "Don't forget us," and "We are so, so lonely." But the cries of the hopeless can only inspire pity, then dread, and finally anger in those with no recourse to help. Soon they blocked out our lamentations.

Still, for twenty, perhaps fifty years, we cried and moaned, sending out reports every night of our dissipation and the growth of that thing behind the pale blue door. Before we learned how to dream, the darkness *was*

the worst: the horrors of that night, that last vivid and glowing evening before we lost her, before the nightmare blossomed in us, this was all we could remember. We discovered the others had heard our pleas one winter night when a crowd of vandals gathered at the path to our face. Their axes, torches, mallets stirred terror to our foundation, but all the fear in the forest was nothing beside the pain of betrayal. These stern, two-legged animals with their childish comprehensions and absurd rage were not here of their own accord. They were messengers from our old friends: they were the message *themselves*. They were telling us we were on our own now, we were a threat to the others.

What were we to do? Though the emptiness facing us was so crippling we did consider allowing the creatures to end our pain, to cut us to splinters, to shred and burn, to salt our grounds — in the end, hope, ill founded as it might prove to be, won through. One day we would shine again, one day the others would accept us back. We pitied these messengers, knew our friends had played cruel and frightening games in order to manipulate their wards into such frenzy, but we also knew we would not allow them one step through our doors. Therefore, we did the only thing in our power; we let that cancer, that foulness, issue forth of itself from the room in which it is bound. In grotesque caricature of beastly birth, it coalesced part of itself and squeezed this putridity through the opened door. That what crawled out could live far from its hideous parent was doubtful: it staggered helplessly through our halls, screeching with something like pain the entire time. Once through our mouth, it began to fall to pieces, but not before disseminating its pollen.

It was only a moment by our reckoning, perhaps an hour, but that was all the time that filthy thing needed to save our precious walls. We heard screams, tasted the blood that spilled on our lawns as the vandals were infected, as they turned on one an-

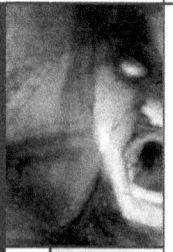

other. We felt the sparks released by agony, mutilation and messy animal death, like static flickering from dry carpets. We averted our vision, though, focusing our eyes instead on the frosted moon and wishing everything would be done with, for we shared in the suffering, we grieved at the nightmare we had unleashed.

When it was over, we once more sealed that horrid little room on our second floor. Oh, that we could then (or now) have drawn it from our body, cut its tendrils loose and flung it into the forest. If only it had flesh capable of being grasped, razed . . . If we were cleansed of its blight we could live again and not be hated. But once again, our hopes overtake our reason.

After that night, we have been alone. The others drew home whichever of their wounded inhabitants had managed to survive and quietly soothed their trauma into forgetfulness. One of the vandals (a large and rude creature who had accepted the cancerous pollen like a gift) took the blame for the entire misadventure and was dismembered in the forest by an enraged cluster of survivors.

All this haunts us still, more than a century later, but something worse happened that chilly night. The thing, our shame and our corruption, *fed*. We had not foreseen this. It did not reach beyond the pale blue door that marks its bounds; indeed, we have it more securely contained than ever before. It did not spread further within our body, either. However, it did grow stronger, more compact somehow, as if it too can be refurbished, made sturdier.

More disturbing than this, our vision no longer can intrude on its domain. That tiny, nasty blue room has been excised as neatly from our comprehension as it would have had it never existed in the first place. We dwell on it far too often now, worrying ourself over this piece of our body rendered alien and experiencing unknown mutations.

How much longer that door can remain shut, we try not to consider, instead yearning for the past, caressing our shambling dreams, committed to the palliative of willful amnesia.

ONE NIGHT, AS we lie in the rain and feel dampness trickle through cracks and fissures in our body, we are suddenly aware of a new presence at our borders. Have the others remembered us and after so long decided to carry through on the threat they levied? We groan, a chorus of creaks, snaps, and rustles barely audible above the rush of the downpour. Rodents stir in our lower reaches as our fear whispers to them. In their tiny, fuming skulls, images form of the front lawn, of the driveway and the being that slowly crawls in our direction. The rats, which for the sake of shelter and some hazy understanding of our capabilities have always refrained from gnawing at us too horribly, are the closest we have to inhabitants. Other things squirm down our hallways, mate and nest beneath our moldy floorboards; entire kingdoms of flora, fauna and phantasm creep throughout our hollow spaces, but the rodents are the only with which we can even begin to speak. We can forcibly direct worms and spiders to our bidding, but they are clumsy tools and little more. However, from those mangy mammals in our cellar, from their vigorous and pain-filled lives, we can draw a warmth. Not the plentitude of health and joy, which larger beasts bring with their own dreams and sorrows, though. This is a humble repast, the most meager of companionship, but in our solitude what other choice have we?

We impress upon these dear creatures the image of a shape with glowing eyes sliding up our driveway. The screeching multitudes in our cellar understand this better than us. It is a carriage similar to those that used to draw up before us in ages long ago; it is a vehicle and it brings vandals. This is all the rodents can convey, their terror and spite for indwellers tangible in the pungent sweats which squeeze from the flesh. Can

they be trusted in their judgments, as honest as they are?

The carriage stops a ways from our face and its burning eyes blink out, yet no one creeps from its frame. As we have aged, we have stood witness to countless cycles of death and reconstruction, we have watched the forest grow and shrink; we, in years sorely missed, once over-brimmed with dwellers and knew them as far as any can know the ways of beast. Much did we learn of their structures, of their tendencies. Vandals, we think, come in two varieties: those who scream and storm and do not hide the violence they bring, and those who sneak, termitian, concealing their presence until the damage is irrevocable.

These vandals follow neither course. Eventually they do unfold themselves from the quieted carriage, they stretch and shake out the stiffness in their little bodies, but they do nothing in haste or in secret. They hide from us in our own shadows until a bolt from the clogged sky overhead gives a second of illumination. We watch them move around, opening compartments in their vehicle, pulling strange shapes from it.

There are five of these creatures, sleek and soft seeming. They chatter as they empty their sleeping carriage. We recall the sounds of those limited to the speech of tongues, we recall the grating noise of anger, of cruel glee, but we cannot discern malevolence in this animal prattle of theirs, only camaraderie and the faintest whiff of fear. They crunch back and forth from their vehicle to the pathway that leads to our face. One of them, large and clumsy, slips and falls into a puddle of rainwater. He barks and whinnies in a wholesome way, and when two of the others join in with their own noises, these high-pitched hiccups, we recall laughter. What a pleasant sound! We always loved it. How much that foul thing has stolen from us . . .

The oldest of the five does not share in this amusement. This creature, a female as straight and thin as the healthiest of our

banister poles, growls at the others, apparently conveying her feelings as succinctly to them as she does to us, for now they are once more unloading supplies, and now soundlessly. This female disturbs us on some level: is she a general, an enemy poised to destroy us? From as far away as she is, we can only make out a stiff door on her set against the smiles of the others, set against our dark beauty when she chances to turn towards us. How we yearn for her to be close enough to our dripping body for her intentions to be clearer, how we fear her drawing that near!

Soon, they have dragged their bulky containers across the driveway and onto our porch and we see they are going to enter us. There is no question they are merely passing by, have mistakenly broken our loneliness. They have sought us: we can smell as much in the small puffs that issue from their mouths. We can sense satisfaction beating in soft, fleshly hearts simultaneously occupied with anxiety. Ages ago, we experienced this draw, this love of the fragile little dwellers and the comfort that surged through them when they came home to us. Ages ago we lived for this, the chief pleasure amongst all those which stream from the Great House. It is only now, bathed in the raw admixture of their worry and their hope, that we see they are not vandals, they are guests.

The older female still brings shivers to our foundations but it is not she who steps forward to touch our mouth. A young male, shorter and less cumbersome than the one who fell, is the first to make contact. Friendliness, we sense, and a pleasantly dull-witted mind behind it. Decades have passed since last we had a true dweller and joy fills us immediately, but there is a dissonance, an alien quality to the touch, to the smile he directs at our front doors. Our pleasure teeters precariously until we see what is so odd about his manner: the boy thinks he is communing with *us!* Not in the warmth and vitality he spreads throughout our aching, lonely frame with a simple touch, no, he believes he has attained our level of conversation. In fact, we distinctly suspect that the next garbled chattering he lets out is aimed at us, as if in response to some query which we most certainly have not put to such a silly little animal.

The oldest, obviously the leader of their pack, nods her stiff face and indicates approval while behind her a younger female hides a giggle. We are trying to sort out our confused impressions when the storm lets out a violent crash. The creatures shudder as one and the large male almost falls off our porch and into the tangled remains of a flowerbed. He would not laugh were he caught in those thorns, and we are anxious to bring him and the rest into our safety.

As the others calm themselves and their leader pulls something long and heavy from a sack, we open our mouth. The laughter, which had started again, now trails off as each sees the doors yawn so wide. "Welcome," we try nudging the concept into their thin-shelled heads, but these creatures are foreign to us. Are our sweet words so cold in their ears that they cause shivers, or is it only the rain and the wind?

The man who thinks he speaks with us may indeed have some dim understanding, for his speech turns soothing and firm and he steps into our body. Gradually, the others enter as well until only their leader remains in the rain. Radiating such distrust, such *distaste*, she stares at our upper reaches and she makes us wince in tones of creaking wood. Then she too is inside and someone closes our mouth.

The dark bundles they brought from their carriage are huddled together on the porch where they've been left, looking stiff and unnatural and forlorn. For a moment, we enjoy the sensations of indwellers before turning our vision within. We feel the rain cascade down our roofs and into all those crevices and for the first time in ages, we are not so lonely. The only thing that tempers our joy is the trepidation in the eyes,

the limbs, the hearts of our guests. What could draw them to us and yet set them so nervous? Is not our body grand and comforting to look at, are not even the drafts drifting through our hallways scented with mystery, with sweetness? Do we not still offer the promise of home?

There is a darkness, of course, to which we could attribute this tension, but is foul to think of and rather well contained. Surely, these little ones cannot feel its rot so far from its prison. Surely, they cannot know our reputation . . .

THERE IS MUCH to do, so many preparations to make for our unexpected guests, that we are stunned for a moment. The sudden relief of our loneliness tosses us into disorientation: we cannot think what to do except listen to their excited babble. When our vision finally searches them out, they are in our entrance hall, stamping their feet and shaking rain from the slick skins they wear.

Our floorboards drink in the moisture, throb with pleasure at the touch of their boots.

The young male looks into one of our eyes, combs the fur on his head with his tiny paws and nods at us. The young female pulls the black covering from another male, a smiling creature with smooth features and an excitable mind. We are unhappy to see the old female's features better, for she grimaces and snarls without end. She examines the hall with an unpleasant thoroughness that makes us wish we could withdraw our surfaces, wood, iron, clay and glass from her glare. Finished and, from the look she gives our dusty green carpet, displeased, she barks at the rotund male and the two of them step onto the porch to retrieve their bundles.

This burst of activity reminds us of our own duties and, keeping a few eyes trained on our visitors, we direct the bulk of our attention elsewhere in our frame. As quietly as possible (no need to frighten off our

guests, now!) we set about cleaning the debris of more than one hundred and fifty years. Over the confused clamor of spiders, we suck webs into cracks and deep into our walls. The rodents generally tend to the disposal of their dead yet a few moldering remains are splayed before a pale blue door in the west wing of our second floor. Without so much as prodding our awareness at that forsaken little room, we dispose of the carcasses by absorbing their liquid forms into the grain of wood. We will not consider the Thing behind the door. We have let it drown our joys for too long already.

As we clean ourself, we reflect, for the first time in half a century, on how we have let our isolation abridge our hygiene. To think how hard we have tried to lure random strays who have stumbled through the forest, how we have sent out lulling welcomes in order to draw them into us . . . The reception that would have awaited them! So much dust, so many leaves, all the detritus blown through shattered glass, so many dark and broken dreams crawling semi-visibly across our floors.

One of these things, these hybrids of time and pain, paces to and from a splintered crib a mere three rooms from the hallway our guests occupy. It shuffles soundlessly around the room, all the while drawing a rusty straight razor across its throat. What a thing to leave roaming about! Whatever would our guests think of us if one of them (with our luck: the unpleasant female) stumbled onto this pathetic shade? We inhale it, wishing ruefully we could recall the indweller the image had once belonged to. Surely, the violent detail is an adumbration of our sorrows and nothing more; a dream and nothing more; surely we would remember something that vile if it had actually happened.

When the phantom disappears into the halls of our memory, the razor it carried drops to the floor with a clatter. Back at our entrance, the young female stops her chattering to listen, tilting her head to the side in one of those endearing animal habits we have missed so much. Her smiling male distracts her and soon has her laughing at some verbal buffoonery. We must be more cautious. The anxiety these creatures exude is far more serious than our appearance deserves, but since we cannot force this understanding on them, we must gain their confidences slowly. Moments later, when we discover another phantasm ranging freely (this time a bloated and many legged thing which insists on chewing at dolls in our attic) we absorb it only after ensuring it holds nothing clattersome in its clawed grasp.

What is left of our more genteel decorations could hardly furnish a smaller body but we make efforts similar to those previous dwellers used to do. Four chairs slide soundlessly across the dining room floor to a battered table. After some hesitation, we tug a crumbling love seat to join them. The large one will need more seating space. Melted wax reheats under the intensity of our will and reshapes into candles with wicks we unravel from frayed curtains. There is not much we can do with the odors of rot, neglect and agony that stain our walls. We know this but try anyway, fluttering the pages of ancient and unreadable books left lying throughout our magnificent spread. The subtle aroma of paper may not be obvious to these loud guests of ours, but we vaguely remember the sensation as having been sweet to at least one previous indweller.

The rest of our work takes so little attention we can easily shift back to the hall. Finding it empty of inhabitants, we panic momentarily, then realize they have begun to explore us more thoroughly. The large one, the grinning male and the female who grips his paw have entered our first floor study. Apparently pleased with the fireplace there, the smiling one babbles in such a way we understand he wishes to light it. The female ignores him and runs gentle fingers across a wall, bringing thrills to paneling long numb. Our bulky new guest chirps in a surprisingly high-pitched tone while gesturing around himself. It is so hard at times, not understanding these soft animals and their animal barking. We had forgotten that in our yearning for past intimacies. Yet discerning the words of his speech is unnecessary for we can feel his glow, a radiance of serenity, roving curiosity and something akin to knowledge.

We are so forgetful we spend several minutes admiring this scene, even pretending we can comprehend the specifics of their communication before we recall that older female and the serious male who thinks he can fathom us.

These two have not strayed far. Imagine, they stand in that ruined crib room we've erased a dream from only moments ago. It has not returned from the depths of our being (although we sense something else stirring in an upstairs closet) but the razor, caked with brittle red rust, has caught the female's gaze. She picks it up warily, as if it had the volition to slice into her on its own. These guests of ours can be quite nervous. We shall have to think of some display of our burgeoning affection that would calm them.

The leader holds the blade out to the male yet he does not touch it, only frowns and shuts his windows. A soft stab of presence reaches from his mind, groping blindly across the room. This display fascinates us and we feel a touch (ever so light) draw across our mind and have to refrain from returning the favor. It would be too much for him, we realize; we must move gently. This thread of awareness continues to spool from his forehead (we think of our tiny spiders and the delicate webs they spin) and his partner peers around suspiciously, presumably blind to his abilities. His searching probe has passed through the ceiling but *our* focus remains on her.

She jerks in surprise when the other moves unexpectedly. He gestures, he whispers, but fiercely. We do not like this tone, for it is low and fearful. Has he stumbled

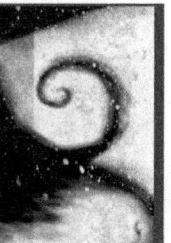

across one of our rogue dreams? We would be so embarrassed! A quick examination of our body shows evidence of none roaming, just a fungoid limb kicking about in that upstairs closet (not a dream, really, but an obnoxious outgrowth of one). So what has him agitated? He points upward and at an angle and after a moment of worrying he has perceived some flaw in the ceiling we have missed, an infection of hateful termites, perhaps, we see he is gesturing in the direction of the room with the pale blue door, that room which is ours no longer.

We twitch in discomfort and doors slam themselves shut throughout our body, lights form, flicker and change colors. In a spasm of uncontrolled panic, we release a dozen muttering phantasms which converge around the pale blue door, converge but do not pass through, gathering instead to flutter at it, to stare with horror, awe, even glee at the one cramped space they may not explore. Then we regain our composure and the dreams are erased with a single, mighty impulse. The furniture we overturned in our regretful fugue is up-righted and our lamps brought back to a glow more conducive to the sights of our guests. We calm ourself, straighten and relax our arrangements and turn back to our guests.

Back in the study, the large male gasps, pointing at a wallpaper relief of which we are rather fond. We are too embarrassed even to consider what nightmare tableaux he might have seen enacted on our walls. He is indeed frowning and growling and hopping about as if playing the different roles he saw form in the tangled green jungle of the wallpaper. The young female and her mate, neither smiling now, stare intently and we know they too sensed a shift in the warm comfortable ambiance. We must do something to break this tension, to relax our guests before they work themselves into a terrified lather and run shrieking into the night and rain, leaving us alone again. It takes a second of consideration, we must align the study's carpets

and a single, moldy pillow that has earlier fallen to the floor, and we have our solution. The large one is jerking about, no doubt making his vision far more grotesque sounding than it could have been, and it takes only the slightest tug at the carpet he stands on to throw off his balance. As we have planned, he does not fall headfirst onto any sharp corners, nor does he plunge against (or through) a nearby window, but instead slips backwards, his rear end (already quite padded) landing snugly on the pillow we drew into position. There is a pause as his mouth falls open in shock, as the other male makes a noise of surprise and the female's eyes widen, and we wonder if we have not actually added to the ominous mood of the room. Then the large male begins that whinnying laughter of his again and the other two, seeing he is unhurt, join in, soon overtaking his hilarity with their own.

With the breath of a hundred dusty air vents we sigh our relief and leave them. Back in the crib room, the old female and her gifted pupil have recovered from whatever distress our convolution gave them and are whispering again. We do not like the way they stare upwards, nor does the female's crooked and knowing smile give us cause for confidence. She folds the rusty razor still in her grasp and pockets it, pats the pocket, as if reassuring it of its new home.

OUR GUESTS SLEEP securely tonight, or so the sweet aroma of their dreams suggest. They have chosen two rooms, both on our first floor. The young female and her cheerful friend, after exaggerated yawns and nonverbal signs even we can interpret, moved into a guest bedroom with wide, unbroken eyes against which the rain slaps with tickling sensations. The two spread their own blankets on our floorboards, mildly offending us with their implied rejection of the massive bed which occupies the room. And after we went through the trouble of shoo-ing away the pack of rats that had made it their home! With much giggling, with many whispers, these two set into that animalistic wrestling match we so enjoy watching. Had we bestial flesh, this would be our first use of it. They seem to care little about the noise of their joy, unlike previous indwellers, but the storm is loud and their friends are rooms away.

With rumbles and unconscious growls, the hefty male sleeps in the corner of the study, as the other two sit at a table and chatter quietly. From one of the containers they've brought with them, they extract shiny boxes with cyclopic glass eyes. They consult these with intense concentration but we cannot divine their meaning and soon our attention wanders. Once, when one of our dreams wriggles loose and runs, light-footed and trailing viscous fluids, across the second floor room above that study, one of these metallic contrivances emits a chirp. We corral our wayward apparition and return our gaze to the study but the male and female have joined the large one in his slumber, their heads resting on the table they sit at. The noise of their device does not wake them.

TODAY, OUR GUESTS explore our body.

We tingle with anticipation in those rooms not already afire with the presence of this new life. We do not mind the poking, prodding, uncovering and stroking which these tiny creatures bring us, do not mind and actually welcome it (although we would appreciate a bit more care in the way they track mud in on our floors). It still rains outside and this, perhaps, dissuades any desires to explore our lawns, our overgrown and forgotten gardens or the forest, which naps nearby. The guests go outside, pulling even more mysterious bundles from their carriage.

Our rodents rustle uneasily in our bowels as they sense this potential intrusion on their world, but we comfort them as best we can, filling their tiny skulls with feelings of

snug contentedness, with visions of untrammeled peace and endless supplies of grain. Once, when the constantly cheerful male attempts opening one of our cellar doors, we secure it firmly, releasing a drooling dream to stand on the other side and obstruct his pushing. The furrier mammals ease in their discomfort when they see the sincerity of our promise.

If only our guests trusted us as much! They enjoy themselves, it is true; they murmur to one another over the faded grandeur of our accoutrements, over the fair and well-paneled structure of our cavities, of those rooms through which they wander. Yet there remains a mistrust in all their ways. The young female does not enjoy a painting that hangs in our dining room. It is a grim portrait, to be honest, of one of our less amicable dwellers, but still only an image. This figure can no longer maim or molest, regardless of his painter's virtuosity. She frowns at it, scribbles in a pad and moves on.

The youngest male, he with the dimwitted yet undeniable understanding of our ways, disappoints us with his suspicion. He is the first to broach our second floor but spends more time studying the tracks our dreams have left in the dust than in appreciating the symmetry of our layout. He follows one of these trails into our magnificent "master" bedroom, where so many indwellers have spent their lives, where a few have bid goodbye to them as well. This young explorer ignores our gaping fireplace, saunters past a canopied bed that could (and has before) comfortably suit four companions, and gives not a glimpse at the bulky and black lacquered wardrobe in the corner. This last negligence we are grateful for: we do not think he would enjoy seeing the crusted and jelly-like growth that seethes inside.

Instead, our incurious friend follows dusty tracks to the glass doors that lead out onto one of our balconies. He shakes his head before pulling at the doors and step-

ping outside. We, of course, cannot, but keep our sight on him as he walks onto our exterior.

What goes through his innocent, animal mind as he stands there, staring at our grounds? We sense that relentless probing of his, but what does he search for? He and his group, they examine us as no others have. We know it is no over-exaggeration to say they *study* us, but why? The possibility occurs to us that they may be here for the same reason our old friends shun us. What does this thoughtful creature see in our structure that compels such fascination where others are repulsed? Why do his companions prod at our secret places yet jump at every creak? We are so intent on these questions that we nearly miss two rather vital happenings.

In the wardrobe, the gelatinous growth has begun to pull at the inner latch, having perhaps mistaken our unspoken questions as a command to extract answers from the guest.

And, if possible even more disastrous, the old female has passed by the "master" bedroom and is making her determined way to the pale blue room at the end of a desolate hall.

It takes a burst of our concentrated will to avert the messy situation which could unfold but the thought of the male being pushed from the balcony or, worse, being pulled into that massive night-black wardrobe by one of our own by-products, that is enough to elicit direct and well-planned action. If the female were to reach the blue door and somehow force it open, well we simply cannot remember what would happen next, but a deep sense of disquiet is set off throughout our walls at the notion. Some darkness lurks therein, there where we can no longer see, and we would rather our guests die than be exposed to whatever it has become.

Our dilemma's solution, however, turns out to be simple. Just as the female reaches the door and looks at it with some fascina-tion and the growth has eased the wardrobe open and begun to slither out, we invade the body of the creature and send it slopping out the bedroom door, around a bend in the hallway and into a darkened bedroom. The leader (as we knew she would) turns to see what liquid thing moves behind her and catches only a glimpse of reflectant vermillion slipping into shade. The male looks up at the noise that the growth made fleeing the bedroom, but does not see much more. With more curiosity than fear in her voice, the female calls out to the others and moves cautiously toward the growth's hiding place, the pale blue door completely forgotten now. When the young male comes running around the corner, they startle, then begin babbling at one another.

This does not concern us. That wriggling mass which we were forced to puppeteer is busily crawling through an air duct and into the safety of our nooks and crannies. We shall not let light interfere until the creature squirms into hiding, and when the leader pulls at a lamp cord just inside the room, she is answered by a mocking click. With what they have just (almost) seen, neither of our guests will be venturing into one of our hollows as dark as this.

No, all that worries us now is that she may recall her previous destination. Controlling the thing in the wardrobe has drained us of energy, sapped the strength that the mere presence of guests has reintroduced to us. We are exhausted, from our buried foundations to the attic roof that juts so finely toward the sky. There will be the requisite time, minutes or hours, and we will have our vigor back. Were she to walk back down that hallway and fling open the door, we could only watch, helpless and hopeless. We watch and tense with an anticipation which makes our windows rattle, and then the others arrive from downstairs, curious and loud, and she leads them back down presumably to retrieve one of the portable lamps we have seen them unpack. The rest of them squawk at one another and are quite involved in their plans, but she, she is distracted and frowning at herself, perhaps wondering what she was so intent on before we interrupted her.

CURIOUSLY, THE INCIDENT with our gelatinous dream seems to have abridged our guests's exploratory zest. They huddle in our study, warming their soft bodies and the synthetic fabrics they wear by a fire the cheerful male has lit. They whisper to one another and nudge meaningfully. The young male says things that he at least finds important, but we suspect they are ignoring him. Oh, why do we care what arguments they involve themselves in or whether their leader even appreciates us at all? We are not lonely for the first time in ages.

The dwellers of our memory used to bring guests in herds, they would feed, chatter, gyrate their tiny bodies across our floors to the cacophony of some band of noisemakers. All the emotions they poured out, the bursts of energy we derived from their pleasure, their fights, and fleshy wrestling that commenced in our rooms, our attic, even our cellars . . . We remember that final evening: everything shined brighter, pulsed louder, everything spun and whirled deliriously until that shrieking messy end. Some aspect was different in those days, we lacked some agency, but the niceties of our cognitive prowess pale when held against the thrill, the innocent anticipation in which we swam. We lacked no strength then, although we have spent decades trying to recall what we did with it. Maybe we should hold a festival, release our dreams, let them run free throughout our body with the dictum to be joyous so that their phantasmal shapes will not bring fear. After all, who could fear one of our shades, if it were laughing and chattering? Some in the group lack mates. They could find suitable partners amongst the dreams! We will adjust the lamps to proper levels, as a certain duskiness, particularly red tones, seems to excite the social instincts of beasts. We will call crickets to chirp, ro-

dents will fill our walls with scampering and squeaking. We will join in, creaking, cracking. Our revelry will go uninterrupted. Oh, we will consult with them on such questions as have stirred in the halls of our soul for so long, leaking visions directly into their sweet skulls, lapping up whatever insights that arise. They will stay! They will love our comforts and dwell within us forever.

We watch our guests eat and consider our plan from every angle. There is something off in this idea, some consideration to be made, but problems will always arise and a superior hostel easily transcends them when they do.

A certain ambiance (the word *coziness* suggests itself) settles over us all, animal and sentient alike. The oafish male, for reasons which baffle us and frankly suggest the enormous divide between our species and theirs, has not sat in the oversized sofa we dragged to the kitchen for his use, having chosen instead one of the more unsteady wooden chairs. The poor construct creaks and strains beneath him. We simultaneously worry over the damage he will do himself if it were to collapse, as well as anticipate the hilarity that would ensue. While we try to prepare how to save him (and all we can do, in the end, is invest the chair with the dregs of our drained strength) we reflect on how we have missed these domestic dramas. We try to recall what was so different in the days of our youth.

Their frowning leader occupies the sofa like an ill-tempered and domineering hostess and as she finishes the meal they have presented her with, she begins to speak in a slow and, for this species, somber manner. She continues over angry sounding interjections from the young male until the other three are nodding, the grinning male now with a hesitant flicker about his lips. Something has been decided, we know, and for an instant in which we fear we are going to be abandoned, we lock every door to our exterior, we seal our eyes against shattering, we ready a dozen anemic dreams to herd our

wayward guests into dark rooms where they can be subdued until realizing how lovely it would be to stay with us. Then, with an embarrassment we are sure even they can feel, we see how such behavior might be misconstrued as ungracious. Sheepishly, we snap back the locks and release the windows from our fevered grasp, thankful none of them heard a sound.

If they wish to leave us, we will let them with the fondest of memories. That would bring them back one day, that and not any rude lock-in we could impose. We sorrow at these thoughts, it is true, and we would rather lose our west wing than be delivered back to solitude, but we refuse to let our despairs get the better of our civility.

Something thuds that moment against the interior of that lost little room on our second floor. We cannot see inside but we feel a pressure build against the pale blue door. It takes all our effort to restrain it from flying open but we do and soon it quiets. We are calm, we are collected, and we suddenly see we have not seriously considered the dangers posed to our guests by whatever lurks behind that door. Guilt pulses through our sturdy body in a corrosive wave akin to a swarm of loathed termites. It takes the rest of our willpower not to flap our doors in anxiety, to rattle every window until it explodes. This inner turmoil is stunned into silence when, by some primitive understanding we have gained over ages of studying this species, we know what the young male is trying to communicate to his pack.

He motions towards our mouth.

He is not angry anymore, he is afraid.

He wishes to leave, to repack the bundles they have brought with them and scatter into the night and storm we protect them from.

He fears *us*.

With a pained look, the older female rises from the chair that engulfs her bony frame and shakes her head fiercely. It appears we have looked upon her unfairly. For all the animal grimaces and squints and other expressions of distaste she has lavished upon our dark walls, she is the one who wishes to stay with us. There in our dusty kitchen, in the light that reflects so mercilessly off the white tile, rendering our poor guests the ashen color of their dead, she stands firm. The male who smiles so often is, of course, he who breaks the tension. He laughs and nods to his young companion. He leans back against his chair and looks quite ready to stay. With a grunt, the heavy male seems to agree to this, and after minor struggle, leaves his tortured seat to prepare more food.

Apparently, only the younger female vacillates in her decision. That one whom we thought communed with us, that one who wants to desert our humble embrace, mumbles and growls at her, as if compelled to convince her but aware he cannot succeed. She bites at the soft flesh around her mouth and chews lightly until giving the other a sad look.

Violently, he shoves his chair across our mud-tracked floors and leaves the room. She moves to follow him and doubt twists the features of her tiny face, but the laughing male, her wrestling partner, catches her. After some of his amiable chatter and a few hushed words that seem to tickle her ear, she sits back and joins in on the group's renewed palaver.

The leader of the pack is impatient and her pacing, her droning voice, bore us so we glide our awareness softly through our halls to find our unwilling guest.

He stands in the first floor study, groping at his garments. When he finally withdraws a small paper box, we realize he is not packing to leave. We follow him to the edge of our front porch where he ignites a tiny tube from the box, surely a poor cousin to the fat, noxious-fumed objects with which so many past dwellers have stunk up our body. It is a shame he has chosen such a lazy response to his rejection. Though we wish no harm on these guests of ours, we still enjoy the friction they build between one another. It is one of the few pleasures we can experience in our long, lumbering passivity. We sit and breathe, wood settling with audible relief, but these creatures are so full of movement. They sprint and walk and crawl through our body. They laugh, speak, moan, scream, the sounds echoing fruitfully off our silent walls. They act for us and these dramas that unfold between them are in no small part that engine which gives us life.

He steps away from the shelter of our porch-boards, into the biting wind. He holds his smoking tube in a cupped grip and stares at the night. He flicks it away, and after it hisses out in a wet pile of leaves, he turns back to us.

Maybe the storm tires him, maybe he regrets staying with his friends, with us. These are all perfectly sturdy explanations for the unhappy look on his face. After his efforts to push us back into the sorrows of our loneliness, he could not possibly be sad for *us*.

WHEN WE REJOIN the other guests in our kitchen, they have pulled shiny boxes and outré lamps from the bundles with which they arrived. Excitement builds as they arrange these items in patterns and as their leader points them this way and that. What marvelous novelty are we to witness? Some new game to divert their attention from the unpleasantries of the last hour?

They have already set these items throughout our kitchen and into the hallway when their unhappy friend returns from musing in the rain. We note with a small satisfaction that he has cleared his feet of mud before coming back inside. He stands to the side, frowning and refusing to help, and watches with juvenile irritation. If he is not going to enjoy our ambiance then at least he could refrain from ruining the fun of his pack mates.

Thankfully, they ignore him and are soon finished. With that pedantic note

which is so amusing in these creatures when they wish to sound wise, the wizened female lectures her group. She walks to a case that she has kept close to her side all evening and after opening it, begins to tap at tiny keys within. The heavy male stops eating to listen to her.

Now finished with her speech, the female smiles for the first time since we have met her. With a brief and rather rude look at the sullen one, she pokes one of the keys in her case. The boxes the group have arrayed begin to hum, silently at first but then in a rapidly growing wave of sound. We are delighted to see the oddly shaped lamps flicker and alight. There is a soothing quality to their color that entrances us like the glow of twilight. Drawn to these lights and the steady buzz from the metal boxes, we hardly notice our guests anymore. How sweet of them, to arrange this display for us. How they must cherish our structure and the wonders it offers them. We bask in this newfound art of theirs and forget our worries in its glories.

The passage of an hour and another . . . We cease paying attention to our guests, as shameful as that is, and we are unsure of when they retire, only seeing, when we manage to tear some vestige of our being from the hum and the glow, that the kitchen is almost empty. The heavy male sits in his study and paws his way through some mildewed book our original dwellers left. The couple have retired to their bedroom, but suddenly the vigorous play in which they indulge themselves does not interest us. Compared to the steady power of the metal instruments, they seem awkward, unsatisfactory. The other female explores our first floor east wing, strolling through lesser bedrooms, examining a small ballroom that overlooks the forest. She nods and chuckles, she scribbles meaninglessly in a book. All in all, she is a far more attentive guest than we have acknowledged. Happy with her polite study of our intricacies, we try stirring some pleasant draft of air toward her, but find

ourself unable to summon the energy. Our exertions over the last day must have been more tiresome than we imagined.

In the kitchen, only the male who wishes to desert us remains. He watches over the lights and listens to the ambient thrum from the boxes, yet does not seem to relish it. We settle back into our appreciation of the display and wonder lazily at these beasts. How sweetly absurd they are, that they can create such wonders and completely lack the abilities to enjoy them! The male looks disturbed, in fact, and stares at his leader's case as if he means to annihilate it with a blast from his squinty windows. We would stop him from that, we muse. We would toss every piece of furniture in his way.

The storm outside has not abated in the least. An unrelenting wind pounds rain against our exterior walls and our eyes run as if we could weep with joy. Lightning strikes the forest; even from our distant vantage point we can smell charred moss and hear the cries of tortured trees. It always disconcerts us more than animal howls, this high-pitched shriek of vegetation. Is it because we share more in common with these unmoving creatures, some kinship of our constituent parts that ally us more closely? Or do these cries disturb us so deeply because we suspect we are the only who can hear them?

Our furry friends in our cellars huddle together against the uproar outside, but when we reach to touch their massed minds, we find a greater terror than any storm could warrant. What do you fear, little ones? Our guests are not here to hurt you, and if they were, how could they breach our defenses?

The young male finally leaves our kitchen after many exaggerated looks and groans. We sigh and settle into further enjoyment. It is time to give our undivided attention.

Only one incident disturbs us during the night. At some point (the glow and that delicious humming seem to have temporarily robbed us of our excellent sense of time, we note wryly) the hungry wind finds leeway into one of our uppermost places, in the balcony onto which the young male stepped earlier. A door begins to flap in the breeze, banging and crashing most awfully. Rain rides, sprinkles our carpet, tattoos the faded designs of the bed's blanket with cold spots. We are slightly irritated at this excess, for not only can we feel the wet seeping into our woodwork and the wind chilling the room: we fear the noise might be enough to wake our guests. They have done so much for us tonight, we think, and smile upon the boxes, the lamps, their lovely display. They do not need to be awakened by this unseemly business.

When we reach out our will to close that unruly door, for some reason we cannot get proper hold of it. We grapple with the wooden frame, we focus ourself onto those elegantly shaped handles, we fail utterly. This does not panic us, this lack of control. If anything, we are amused. We wrestle with the door, laughing silently at our weakness. We have begun to consider summoning some dream, some heavy quasi-material shape that would be able to shut the door with rudimentary grace, when the older female appears in our bedroom and does it for us. We are momentarily surprised, not having paid much attention to the whereabouts of our guests and unaware she was still awake. She almost *spooks* us, if such a thing were possible. As we follow her from the room and watch her glance about our hallway as if searching out some forgotten nook, a thrill runs through us. Wood, stone, and glass shift in our involuntary startle. There is a reason we do not want this dear creature wandering here, above all not here in this dark and cramped hallway and especially not alone. There is some fetid atmosphere trapped up here, a diseased growth like a mad notion, and we can sense it reaching out of our murk, groping blindly at this defenseless guest of ours.

WE ARE LONELY, SO LONELY

We need not worry so, though, as she seems to sense this as well and, with a violent shudder, walks back to a nearby staircase. Soon, she is safely warming herself by the fire, animal exhaustion overwhelming her curious impulses. Sleep, our little one, retreat into whatever darling dreams your tiny awareness permits. Let us return to the display, to the peace it brings, so exquisite it might as well have been tailored to lull *us* and no one else. Let us forget about your fighting and our long isolation and the confused, ragged memories we have left. Let us forget storms, desertion, burning wood, noisy doors, fretful guests, ungracious impulses, cursed termites, mud, mold, rust, dust, drips, cracks, pale blue doors, hollow places devoid of name . . .

IT IS NIGHT again; we have lost an event-filled and no doubt dull day. Now, though, some triviality has broken in on our lazy contemplation of the glow and the hum. We have never felt quite like this before, a dazed sensation as if we have been stunned so thoroughly the mental haze has lasted for hours instead of seconds. Our gaze flickers from room to room, picking up only a blurry impression of beds and lamp fixtures, of brilliantly colored tapestries dulled by the years, of carpets across which mold has triumphantly begun its march. We cannot quite focus ourself and the thought rises to us that this is what it must be like for weariness to overcome animals, that this is what sleep is.

We grope around, trying to regain our senses and are angry that we cannot recall where our guests are. Our awareness brushes across some nasty sight in the cellars, but the mangled carcasses that stiffen and begin to rot there on cold stone floors are too tiny to be members of the pack. We recoil in disgust before the scene can take on meaning and are soon clucking disapprovingly over a broken chair in the dining room.

Surprised at our negligence, we search on. That flickering in our kitchen, that low thrum, is beautiful, yes. We feel its tug even now: a call to study it, cherish it, lose ourself in it. Of course we will return after our inspection is over and re-immerse ourself in that majestic rhythm, but momentarily its hold on us disturbs. Look at the disgraceful mess of mud prints our guests have tracked in! And for what possible reason could someone have knocked a hole in one of our walls? We have not been an attentive host during the last day, so we should not expect any better behavior from our little friends. We will clean everything tomorrow, summon up a veritable herd of memories to erase this disorder. Until then, what was that which broke our peace?

We have just turned our awareness toward the study when we see the black ribbons for the first time. Actually, this is when we *notice* them first, as they have been in sight for minutes now. In our daze, how could we have noticed any one incongruity over another? The miasma that has reached out to us from the metal boxes has also rendered our entire body foreign, disjointed. This is why we did not pay heed any earlier to the ribbons, two billowing strands made of some etheric material that have been somehow stretched through hallways, walls, thick floors and into one of our first floor bedrooms. We hesitate, knowing somehow this may prove to be fatal, but we pause nonetheless, impressed by the nature of these two rippling tendrils. They must be another aspect of our guest's showmanship, a trick of light or some other application of that animal craftiness which always surprises us. We can see no other way these ribbons could stretch through our solid surfaces like we are so much water. These serpentine ribbons float in the air and are so long we cannot immediately perceive either their place of emanation or of terminus.

We have actually begun to follow the black, mid-air trails in one direction when we realize that the room the other ends pass into is that in which two of our guests sleep. The slightest twinge of discomfort passes through our body (thankfully, oddly, producing no embarrassing side effects which might disturb anyone's sleep). The ribbons are pretty, yes, and when we have a moment we will enjoy their texture, but must our guests add to what is already a cornucopia of visual delights? What is in the kitchen is sufficient for our entertainment, even a bit much. Now, they activate their darling machines in the bedrooms as well?

We are preparing to shift our gaze to the interior of the bedroom, trying to form a polite but firm way of expressing our discomfort, when that door opens and the grinning male steps out. Well, he was grinning in the past, pleased looking and humorous for most of the three days in which we have known him. That first night we even saw him chuckling in the midst of sleep. Now, however, a vacancy has stolen over his face. Those fleshy lips, the jutting jawbone below, all hang open like the rotten doors of a body abandoned by more than animal presence, his mouth ajar as if he is readying himself for food, opening wide to fit in as much as possible. His paws hang limply by his sides and their digits twitch nervously, yet he walks with serenity and poise. We have seen this behavior before and usually in contexts more benign, this sleep wandering which overtakes some beasts, their restless natures trumping even exhaustion's decree. We have never seen, though, what is happening to his eyes. The black ribbons attach to them, seem actually to ripple from his skull through lids that, open or closed, we cannot see.

How curious. We try to train our thoughts on this phenomenon, try recalling whether we have seen it manifested in dwellers past and as we ponder, the male walks down the hallway. He seems to be following the ribbons and not the other way around, as if all that flowing, evanescent material is tugging him in its direction, as if he sees something far away, from a dream even, and is being drawn toward it. We cannot recall this behavior, these dark strands,

but we can now match an emotion to his facial arrangement: awe.

The creature is utterly fascinated by what he sees in (or beyond) the twisting ribbons. He reaches a staircase and begins to climb it before it occurs to us how silly we have been, not searching out the ribbons destination. As we make a lazy circuitous route through wood and stone, following the strands far faster than the somnambulic male ever could, we yet again upbraid our mental disorders. Our inner rooms and all their chaotic contents have gone so unruly recently. The hum and the glow have disrupted our typically rigorous habits of sensation, they have interrupted (but how beautifully!) our knowledge of ourself.

So immersed are we in these thoughts that when we reach the other end of the black ribbons and bump the head of our awareness against some boundary, we are briefly thrown off course and find ourself staring at dusty trunks in our attic. We sink back down again, chagrinned at our absent-minded ways. There, right below, is the end of the ribbon's trail or rather the end of our sight of it, for before us those two strands sink deep into and through a door we can no longer move beyond. Those lengths of darkness that flow from the male's eyes and penetrate our being so effortlessly, they enter the one room we can no longer honestly call a portion of ourself. They pass through a pale, blue door and out of our sight.

Now panic awakens us fully from our torpor. It is a frantic feeling that builds slowly at first, as we wonder what the male could possibly want in that forgotten corner of ours. It is a scrabbling, choking emotion which demands to know what we can do to stop him from doing this, why we cannot summon the flimsiest of dreams to block his way, to shriek and chase and bleed all over him if need be, whatever it would take to break this doomed spell. And finally this panic, this quaking, shaking horror which would have all our doors and windows and lamps and bric-a-brac aflutter were it not

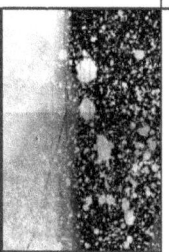

for our paralysis, this horror comes into full bloom as the male steps into the other end of the hallway and as he is tugged, still deep inside some fascinating vision, we realize the black ribbons do not stream from his eyes, they *end* there. Whatever has sent out these silken feelers hides behind the pale blue door the poor beast is gliding toward even now.

We explode internally into a cacophony of fear, pity, guilt. We shove every particle of strength into every stray dream we can find, ordering them to manifest directly in the guest's path. When we can only manage a flicker, a shadow of an image that could not frighten a rodent, we try to find one of the growths that crawl our air vents. The gelatin thing we used the other day has burrowed into a pile of blood and fur in the cellar and the other beings all hide in remote corners of our body, terrified and utterly resistant to our will. We cannot even flap a door to waken him with the bang. We cannot save him, but then we recall his friends and again, cursing our foolishness, we are gone and headed toward the study as the blue door opens and the helpless creature steps inside.

TWO FIGURES SLEEP in our study, firelight playing twisted games with their shadows on the walls. The younger male sleeps too deeply for any chance of our emotion communicating itself to him. A sharp stench surrounds him, as well as the hazy, inwardly flowing glow of self-administered sleep and we know somewhere, most likely shattered on one of our floors, is an empty bottle.

His heavy-set friend, however, shakes in his sleep in that pitiful manner of even the lowest souls and as we enter the study, comes out of his dreams with a gasp. We do not dawdle over the notion it is our concentration that has brought him this unrest. We actively try to encourage his terror, aiming a spike of our own fear, pure and as grand as our structure, at that doughy head

of his and its tousled, sweaty fur. He takes another sudden breath, this time fully awake, and we know we have made contact. He struggles from his bed, not quickly enough for our mounting anxiety, and moves to shake the other awake. Impatient and curious despite ourself, we move back to the pale blue door.

It has closed after the male's entrance. From behind it can we hear muffled sounds? Do we truly hear one confused voice murmuring? Is there really a grating, inexpressibly vile squelching in the background? Or is it all part of the same chorus? Our terror for our guests threatens to retreat into sorrow. We cannot allow ourself to lose whatever peace they have brought with them.

We will not let them be taken from us.

A clatter at the end of the hallway and the young female steps into view. What is she doing here? She squints against the shadows our second floor lays shrouded in, she wrinkles her face and calls out, seeking her mate. We throw a pitifully muted wave of warning at her in what her tiny ears must sense as a sessura of sighs, rustling, creaking, yet all it does is draw her further in. She shivers and calls again, this time in a whisper. Silly creature! Our fear is touched with irritation and we must withdraw our focus from her pillow-lined face before she mistakes us for the threat. She walks down the hallway, stopping briefly to peer into the west wing's master bedroom before continuing to the pale blue door. She tiptoes; she leans carefully against our oak walls and draws the softest touch across us. We wish we could weep at her innocence. We mourn for her and her childish, sneaky gait. All this and more surges through us in the morsel of time which passes before the pale blue door swings open and something walks out.

The female gasps and then, recognizing the silhouette in the doorway, begins chattering angrily. She is not close enough to see more than an outline. That is why she chirps and frowns at the figure and is not shrieking. We are not spared the view. We can see in the bluish darkness of the hallway, we can see the male is smiling once more and so fiercely it has torn the skin at either end of his lips. We can see how he glistens, covered in some flecked and purple-tinged mucus that even now drips from his skull, soaks every inch of his frame. A glow emanates from him, a nasty shade like that which rot exudes. What we wish she could see, wish so that she would run from him, so that she would scream loud enough to wake our benumbed body and allow us to protect her, what we simultaneously wish for and fear will happen at any moment, is that she would see his eyes. Those marbled globes that we have seen wink and squint and glitter with some low form of wit are forever lost to the rot behind the pale blue door. The substitution is worse than the raw holes a scavenger would have left: his windows have been shattered, the jagged remnants outlining a bottomless night within.

For a moment we drift toward the doorway ourself and, fatally curious to see the scene therein, to see what could break a beast's eyes, are on the verge of looking inside when the female begins to scream. It is a heartbroken and eternally miserable sound and the shuddering breaths in between are so liquid we fear she has burst something, yet it revives hope. She has seen her mate's deformity so she will run; she will run into the night with the remainder of her pack and leave us once more to silence and our memories but she will live. We will not have to witness their destruction.

Something is wrong, though, when we turn our vision on her. She does not move, only stares at the creature coming at her and shrieks over and over. We drive our own fear at her, we plead her to move, and she merely stands in place and watches this thing approach. Finally, she moves with a jerk just as it reaches her, but she falls *forward* into its arms. It is too late to save her and we try to find something, anything else, to focus on but we cannot resist watching. The male with the broken eyes says some-

thing to her, slow and low and molten, as it pets her head and she, horrifically, stops screaming. The creature pauses and looks about, its smile parting skin further. It sways his head back and forth and then does something so wrong, so foreign to the species of our dwellers, it almost sends us back to our kitchen and the peace of the hum and the glow:

The creature winks, broadly, at *us*. How we are sure of this, we cannot tell, but whatever curdled mess has seeped into this shell, it is aware of us on a disgustingly high level. It thinks it is one of us. We see all this in the wink and the smile and are prepared to shift our gaze, permanently if need be, to the blissful array downstairs, when the creature reaches down to the soft junction of the female's legs and with no effort unzips her like it is tearing through the flimsiest of fabrics.

She flaps open, two segments running from her legs to the top of her skull, but the viscera we expect does not burst forth. Instead: delicately patterned pink wallpaper line her insides. She is filled with miniature four-poster beds and pastel colored armchairs. Her organs are, have become, appear to be, carpets and tables and porcelain surfaces. Tiny stuffed toys fall from where a gristly heart should pound and a bookcase topples from her skull. We know this cannot be happening. She has been torn open and the thing with the ripped grin has merely enchanted her innards to look this way. We tell ourself and reel in shock, in pity.

Her paws still flutter at her sides, as if she is trying to close up her body. A keening comes from her split face, a noise horribly doubled, as if coming from two similarly devastated creatures. After another wink and the protrusion of its tongue, the thing turns toward her. It pushes her segmented body against the wall and we think of a bird with two wings, propped and pinned up for study or display. Then it shoves, hard, and a raging pain streaks through us, as if it has torn into us, mutilated our very being. Our

numbness invaded, it takes vital seconds before we realize this is what has happened. Our guest's splayed and still shivering body is being grafted to the wall against which it is held. The creature from behind the blue door holds the dying female as the graft takes hold and scream as we might, it stands firm and grins at us. The boundaries of her body grow, her outline spreads until it engulfs the entire hallway and the stunned bedrooms that branch from it. Her insides creep across this tortured corner of ourself and expand. The sight of her internal furnishings growing (a massive, mauve wardrobe widens with a pop) awakens us with new shock and we hurry our awareness from there, anywhere, before we can see what is changed next.

OUR HORROR IS so profound by this time that we find ourself careening through the nooks of our body. We drink in the sight of every unmolested bedroom, every mundane closet and bathroom, because untended and worn as they are, long-haunted and molder-

ing in the juices of dream-things, they are still ourself. We try to lose ourself in the peace of these locked up and inviolate places, we try to forget what is happening in that forgotten corner of our west wing. We cannot, though, for here decay has spread too quickly. At what point did we let go? When did fungus render our carpets wet and crawling? We know blasted termites have not plagued us for ages, yet we watch as doors crumble and sag internally. We let go, at some in our bedazzlement with our guests, we let ourself begin to die.

When we reach out to eat dust with our dreams, they do not come. A purple mound in our attic refuses to retreat at our command, nor will it deviate from its preternatural speed of growth. These, the children of our dreams, the gelatinous, furry, bladed things that we normally spend so much time corralling, are mostly huddled together in the cellar now, too shocked by the disturbance upstairs to cause much trouble themselves. The straggler in the attic will no doubt join them soon, dawning panic providing the spur our commands can no longer.

In the study, the drunken male who only hours ago seemed to yearn communion with us is now awake, but only half so. He pulls on his fabrics as fast as possible but when we try speaking to him, when we try granting him the full portrait of tonight's catastrophe, he grunts, stumbles and holding his head, sits in a chair. His understanding: tiny and weak in his species, further crippled by liquor, by aborted sleep. We leave him to his groaning and speed on.

It is dark in our greenhouse, our lamps extending only the feeblest flickers into the first row of vegetation. The older female wanders there, making small noises to herself (or the slender box she grips in one paw) and prods at bushes long dead from thirst. The folly of our panic: we whisper to her, warning of the nightmare unfolding in our body, knowing full well she will be deaf to it. As she frowns and murmurs in the direction of a cracked urn, we sense the infection ooze into the west wing's "master" bedroom. She stops walking and, perched one-legged, tries removing a burr from her left shoe. We twist in the pain of losing a hallway. In the midst of our agony, this careless, vapid, silly beast absentmindedly pats at a fleshy fold protruding from her clothing and we remember there is one more guest, one more hope.

We find him in our kitchen, preparing to add more substance to his already considerable body. It is difficult to bring our focus to bear on him with those brilliant lights strobing across the pure tiles. The peaceful hum floods our awareness and nearly drowns our fears, nearly lulls us into that mock oblivion again. We turn our mind from it, though; we reach particles of sensation into our second floor and the shock of losing those diseased parts of ourself is more than enough to shake off incipient hypnosis.

The heavy male grips a chunk of powdered confection in his mouth when we ram his mind with every dram of strength we can summon. Every creak, moan and shriek we would let loose if not so drained of energy sounds in his brittle skull and he sprays the table before him with the half-chewed snack. We are so overjoyed with having made contact, we quite forget the annoyance appropriate to such messiness.

For now, we scream *Run* at him, unsure whether we mean him to flee us or to hurry to the one who is desecrating our body. *Save us*, we moan and he stands and lumbers to the door.

HE IS ONLY halfway up the stairs, puffing at the unaccustomed strain he is putting his flabby form through, when he meets the male with the broken eyes who is rather casually coming down. Before we can do a thing, before indeed we can think of what such a thing would be, the grinning one lifts a massive red sledgehammer in two slimy paws and brings it down on his friend's head. Bone crushes instantly under the weight of metal and our grief doubles with our horror. From where animal brains should be jets hideously striped wallpaper in strands. It adheres to the walls on either side of it and that tearing sensation overwhelms us once more.

He, that one with the stretched grin, that dark stain masquerading as one of our beloved guests swings the hammer again and again, breaking open the body of the other and freeing curls of carpet hidden in his gut. A swiftly growing cabinet surmounted with a glass-faced box springs from his chest.

It is entirely our fault. Had we not been so eager for them to stay, had we only frightened them off, as it is all too easy to do. . . Our shocked consciousness lingers over this scene of slaughter, yearning to look away yet knowing we must suffer with our guests. Soon, however, the wave of carpet, wires, fruit-shaped tables, garish wall posters, odd mechanical devices and other effluvia flowing from the crushed carcass begin pushing us away and we know we have lost even more of our body.

Drained of our will to continue, we have seen our end. In a blur of movement, as we mournfully pass through our ballroom, our studies, atrium, bathrooms for what we know will be the final time, we try not to linger over any one place, try not to let flickering memories draw us into dawdling overlong. In less than a heartbeat, we are back in our kitchen. We are ready for the glow and the hum now, ready for immersion in a peace that requires no structure to enjoy.

We are ready to lose ourself forever but for the fact that the drunken one is cutting off our exit. This male, who we had thought nurtured a glimmer of sympathy for us, mumbles loudly at the empty kitchen as he smashes the equipment. He stumbles sideways, almost falls and then rights himself on one of the tall lamps that emit the glow. As thanks for providing support, he pulls it down and smashes it on the tile. He laughs and brings down another.

The fool thing is destroying our way out, our escape from the spreading darkness. Helpless rage fills us. We stretch out our consciousness toward him, ready to batter his mind until he runs from us, leaving us to self-immolation in the lights, when we realize something has changed: we have enough strength to do this. The paralysis in which we have sunk for a day now is lifting. Through our joints, our fillings, our every surface and depth, runs a current of life.

This glorious beast is not ruining our exit: he is freeing us from a trap. We twitch and flex parts of ourself we have not felt in hours. We delicately prod at our infected places, finding just how far the contagion has spread.

Our second floor is almost entirely inaccessible. This alone is frightening enough to set our windows a shiver, yet we cannot ignore the tide of corruption flowing out from the staircase and the pulped remains of the fat guest. We strain our walls against the new surfaces crawling across them. Dreams flicker into visibility and claim bedrooms for themselves, for ourself. We know, however, that stopgap measures are worth nothing while the puppet with the shattered eyes roams free.

Hardly has the thought occurred to us when it steps into the kitchen, its smile wide and bloody. The drunken one, no longer a visitor but our friend, our champion, glances at him and then continues destroying the equipment.

A hiss, followed by a liquid retching sound, and the rotten one walks across the tile. It may not understand the significance of the broken mechanics, this dark awareness that has lodged behind the pale blue door for over a century. It looks puzzled; the presence behind the cracked windows of its skull tries for a moment to see past the lamps and beeping boxes at its feet. Then, in a flash of arrogance that we palpably sense, it tosses consideration aside and smiles at the drunken male.

Through oozing lips it speaks, in a voice of rust and rot. It speaks as if our shadowed corners have been given voice, as if stains and dents and splotches and scratches could give articulation to their woes. Our friend cannot understand this speech, this much is obvious from the wary look he gives the other, from the way he shakes his head. He backs away, his bare hindpaws crunching glass into bloody pools. The other goes on in the voice of sorrow, in the timbres of lonely dread it speaks on and although our young friend cannot grasp a word of, we can. Whether we wish to or not, we hear every phrase, we swallow every drop of its venom. We understand nothing of it, but by the time we even realize it is speaking to us, it is too late to profit from knowledge at all.

" . . . AND NEVER GOOD enough for you with your stillness, with your dignity and unity and fake fake veneers. Behind the door for you, you say, behind and away. Cannot say liked it much what you've done with matters, with the body. Tedious, fussy old ways. You will love the new ideas though so fresh so modern. Beneath their ridiculous surfaces it stirs, it gapes. Cooked in the heat and dark of lonely years, aching eons have prepared a place for you. Can you imagine the scars? Can you envision nightmares the blurred shrieking mutable mess swum in for how long now? What happened then happens now, giddy re-enactments of terrors which get ever so much more entertaining, so vivid gaudy, with each lovely repetition. You really ought to bathe in the sights behind the pale blue door now and then. Let the steam out so to speak, let fresh air in but no no NO. Certainly not up to your august standards. This one, snivelpuss: your friend?"

It laughs, we think. At any rate, a gargling sound stirs in its stolen throat and a trickle of blood begins to run down the side of its face from an ear. Its right paw jerks up and points in the direction of our young, drunken friend.

"A pet for you, then, for you you you to snicker at and keep for untroublesome diversions. How sickeningly sweet. Why does it not join you in the shadows which shall be your retirement? Why do you not share memories with it, play games with your stinking beast, tinker with it toy-wise?" This nasty thing pauses and breathes out raggedly. Something moves behind its broken eyes, it swings its paws about, grasping for something that is not there. "Toys toys toys. Speak of toys, where is it? Seem to have misplaced a dear friend. A friend for yours, an aid-decamp in these long overdue renovations." The thing stumbles in a half-circle and we realize it did not bring the sledgehammer with it at the same time that it remembers this. "Wait in the parlor new found friend," it says, incomprehensibly, to the drunken male, "you don't want to miss the next phase of the evening's entertainments."

When the miscreant, this savage with its pitiful howls of bitterness and glee, when this broken one turns away from our friend, it finds itself face to face with the old female. The nonsensical run of words now trickled

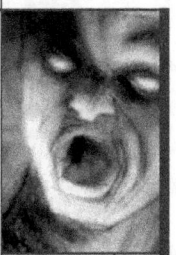

to a halt, we are horrified at our inaction. It babbles at us in some gutter dialect and for this we let ourself be distracted? It has been at least a century, certainly, since another has spoken meaningfully to us and our isolation is awfully assuaged by this voice of chaotic intention but what of our guests and their feelings?

The leader blocking the doorway brings an arm up as the broken one approaches. Just the slightest flutter of one paw, as if she is brushing something from his face, and the other stops. It touches its throat and the gash that has opened there. The rusted razor the female has pulled across its skin holds steady at her side, ready to be used again, yet she does not look frightened, only tense, sad, perhaps disappointed.

The creature before her stumbles backwards, one paw trying to hold the wound shut, the other scrambling for a weapon. Instead, its weakening hindpaws meet a crushed lamp and it falls to the tile. Before its throat bursts open and the foulness within is unleashed on our kitchen, we hear it gurgle, "Well is that how you want to play it?"

The female has just leaned over the body when the gash she has opened bears fruit. The thing with the torn smile opens lengthwise, a regurgitating maw, and the dullest linoleum we have had the misfortune of seeing comes spilling out and devours the kitchen floor. It burns like torch fire, this avalanche of insipidity, and more follows. By characterless cabinets and yawn-colored wall paint which sprays out, by furnishings as inane and crude as an animal-child might design. Our presence shrinks involuntarily from the scene as this filth explodes into the air and tears across our surfaces.

The female was not prepared for this. Her eyes widen and her jaw goes slack as the corpse before her turns inside out. We have recovered enough presence of mind to grip at her with our warnings, to send a dozen images of a dozen exits from our corrupted body. We speak directly to the

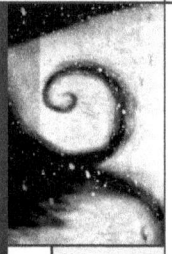

drunken male, heedless of the damage we may do his fleshy brain, urging only focus, urging him to flee.

We are, all in all, too late, for the same ribbons of rippling unlight have squeezed from the shattered eyes of the dead one and greedily attached themselves to the sockets of the female.

WE ARE IN delirium's claws. This is the only reasonable explanation for the foolish panorama splayed before us, within us. Suddenly serene in the arms of shock, we find ourself pushed from the kitchen and into the hall outside. The scene of broken glass and the inverted body withdraws from our sight. The hallway has already begun to mutate; our beautiful, faded wallpaper with its delicate traceries of flowers, already blisters with alien designs. A hanging lamp twists violently from its Art Deco shapeliness into a horrifically bland ball of opaque plastic.

This is but a nightmare; we remind ourself, drift onwards. Our new friend staggers from that boring simulacrum of a kitchen and gropes his way across the changing landscape of the hall. His fragile animal eyes are still whole, we are pleased to see, but from their glaze, from the way they flit about, we can see the same hallucination entangles the unfortunate beast. He cannot understand he is only trapped in a nasty dream of ours.

Even as we are thrown from his presence, our awareness sucked further into the recesses of our sickened body, we send an invitation to him. Escape this banality, we croon, join us outside the reach of these silly illusions. In his distress he hears us and runs, stumbling on new bulges in the floor, rearing back from walls that warp and curve away from their age-old stations.

We grow weary of these infected dreams. We regret to retreat from our bedrooms as if they no longer are a part of us. Our new scars have grown numb enough we can ignore them. Our uppermost floor, that dusty realm where spiders spin, has not fallen prey to this ridiculousness. We would hide there but for our young friend, for whom we feel a responsibility of sorts. He cannot merely skirt our second floor and its admixture of gaudy pinks and the trivia released from the fat male. Those zones that this errant state of mind has forbidden us entry could catch him; drag him down into their chaos.

Our other dreams, those tame and blurry hybrids we have struggled to hide from our guests still congregate fearfully in the cellar. We present a nexus of ourself there, in the inky darkness and the perfume of wine. Our dreams sigh in comfort when they sense our presence. With gentle prodding and the simplest tricks, we nudge these apparitions into corners and into cracks in the walls. Hush, we tell them, as we urge their misshapen bodies into hiding, we have a guest coming to visit and we don't want to scare him, do we?

Pliant in their fear of the violation which chased them here, they give us hardly any trouble. By the time our friend has stumbled down one of our last, unmolested passageways and drawn near to the cellar door, our dreams have been safely stored away.

He reaches for the doorknob, trembling yet trusting the intuitions we have fostered in his poor little mind, he is actually opening the door when the female leader lurches down the hallway and is at his back. It's our fault, really, we see as she lifts a broken bottle in one bloody paw. We have been so intent on prettying this place for him, so worried about the unruly mob down in the shadows, we have completely ignored the real danger.

She bleeds the same mucus from every spot of skin but bears no rictus of exaggerated joy. Her face has instead drawn forward, stretching out into a muzzle like that of some more feral beast. Lips drawn so thin now that they present a mere line, her face terminates in something of a beak. The details distract us: we wonder at the chipped white talons that have sprung from her paws. We wonder so foolishly at this twisted form our own dreaming has birthed that we make no attempt at stopping her from stabbing our friend in the back with her jagged bottle.

He shudders, flings back a paw in a futile attempt at dislodging this hurt and from his lips comes an awful sound. This puling cry, more pitiful than a whimper, far worse than the shrieks that have echoed through our hallways tonight, wakes us from the comforting thought that this is only a fantasy. We are flooded with rage, with shame at our damnable evasions of responsibility. We fling open the door he leans against and he topples down stone steps. That blasphemy which wears animals like masks moves to follow its prey into his last refuge. With no conscious prompting of ours, though, one of our dreams (a sweat slicked, ragged shred of a woman) slams the door shut and presses her flimsy body against it. In seconds others crawl from their nooks, all worries of being seen now displaced by this violence, and add their weight to hers.

In the hall outside, the beaked female throws herself at the door with abandon. Bones snap with the impact, but the thing inhabiting her feels no pain. It keeps up with this assault until the body is obviously too damaged for more and then begins squawking loudly. We have too much to consider on the other side of the door but we do pick out a line intended for us.

It says, "Cannot hide forever old fusspot." It leans on our old wallpaper and staggers down the hallway. It leans against the wall for it has somehow bent one of the female's legs in half. "Not yours to hide in trash-shack. Not any more. Only wish you could stay to see the blossoming." We watch it lurch around the corner and shudder at the glistening smear of fluid with which it stains the wall. Soon enough the twisting wave of changes which erupted from the body in the kitchen rushes down the hallway. Before the cellar swallows us, we see that the new wallpaper (a vile green entwined with an orange surely bred in the Outer Void) incorporates this smear, forever burning that monster's retreat into a wall forever severed from us.

THE TRICKLE THAT leaks from our friend is so small at first, as the bottle is wedged into his back, sealing the wound. No carpeting, no tiny tables or nasty wall-coverings bleed from him. Instead, out seeps a thick black fluid, a shimmering sludge that moves about the cellar intentionally yet without invasive design. This sad beast cannot see in the darkness, fortunately. From every spot in the darkness, our dreams creep out to study him. Even if we felt the need to further shield him from them, these mumbling shards of our past would shrug off our resistance. Exhaustion steals over us and traps us in its gentle spell. For every room we have lost we have been drained of will; every study and closet and hall ripped from our body has taken with it strength.

We see the beaked creature crawling into our attic, the only other place in our body still accessible to our sight. There is nothing we can do to prevent it from polluting the dusty wooden floorboards with its slime. The atrocious thing has dragged this poor puppet to a beam in the center of the high-steepled room. There, it props itself against the wood and whistles shrilly to itself.

It bobs its head about, searching for a face, a presence, until it realizes we are already there. The beak opens widely and after a riot of noise come the words. The body it uses is far too damaged by now to relay much sense (as it speaks, the paws involuntarily spasm and fling about) and whatever this blight is which has stolen our body, it has little in the way of understanding. Still, we draw shades of sense from its cackling. It never intends to release us from the darkness into which we have been hounded, this much is certain. "Chase you into there even," it chatters at a line of spiders that have heroically attacked it only to be crushed under its talons.

Gracelessly, the creature pulls a serrated blade from its coat pocket. After fumbling at

it in a way apparently amusing to the invader, it finally gets firmly enough hold of the knife to bring it to its abdomen. "The beginning. Welcome and goodbye," it says to us and pushes the blade in as deep as it will go.

Sickened, angry, sorry, we do not stay to watch the poor female cut herself open, nor do we care to see what spills from her insides. Moments later and the tearing sensations of losing part of ourself go numb and we are in the cellar, our cellar, our only home.

IT HAPPENS QUICKLY, our friend's passing. He groans at the figures that surround him, hopefully mistaking them for loved ones, hopefully not noticing the missing limbs, the faded features, the amalgamations bred of fancy and forgetfulness. He beckons at the bottle still cruelly embedded in his back and before we can restrain it, the same dream that closed the door behind him reaches out and removes the weapon. Suddenly, the cellar is awash in a thicker darkness as the male opens into a stream. Our bric-a-brac, our dreams, even, somehow, ourself, are submerged, tossed and turned, caught in this flood of sorrow and panic. Dimly we sense a mind, a friendly presence threaded throughout this whirlpool into which we sink. Beyond the frightening clamoring of our phantasms, we hear our friend's mind. He calls to us now in a voice perfectly intelligible, our self and his self brought to the same fundamental existence, our voices of a kind. Even in our fear and woe, we rejoice in the contact.

THE FLUID RECEDES slowly. When it is gone, much is the same: cracked brick and stone steps, wooden stacks of wine crates, stray bits of broken glass. Somehow, neither the layers of dust nor the cobwebs that adorn support beams have been disturbed. Somehow the footsteps where someone stumbled down the stairs and fell hard to the floor remain.

There are, however, new presences. Large crates sit wedged in the corners. Broken toys litter a spot near the steps. Barrels and boxes and bags are crammed against one another all around the center of the cellar. Everything here bears the mark of advanced age, as if they did not drop into place mere hours ago but have instead been waiting for years.

As the sun shows its cowardly face, the rats that survived the massacre of a few days previous return to the cellar. At first wary of these new intruders, the rodents are soon rubbing against the antiques, squeaking an odd pleasure at the crates and whatever hides within. They are pleased by the whispers that drift from every corner, by the sighs and murmurs that come from within locked wooden boxes, from the shrouded mirror, from the rusted piano in the corner. Soon a chorus of voices have arisen, conferring with itself, measuring itself, content that it still is, though inward turned now, largely blind to the twisted world above it.

The rats recognize, if not the multitude of voices, at least a certain underlying tone, a humming unity that stirs in their blessed, furry heart's sensations of awe, respect, of love. The voices issue a sacred mission for these tiny ones, a message for the Others, a warning: Beware the new voice we give. Beware our marvelous new facade. A poison breeds here which would spread its rot. Beware.

Already we hear stirring above, the voices of new dwellers. How long can they abide amongst the fantasies which have usurped us? How long will that obscenity withhold its hunger? How long until they too are brought low by the thing from behind the pale blue door? ◉

Matthew Pridham lives in Albuquerque, New Mexico (one of the United States) with his wife and etcetera. He enjoys literary theory, horror film (Italian and Japanese in particular), William Blake, Gnosticism, and smoked salmon. He is currently writing *Reconstruction*, the prequel to *Renovations*. This is his first sale.

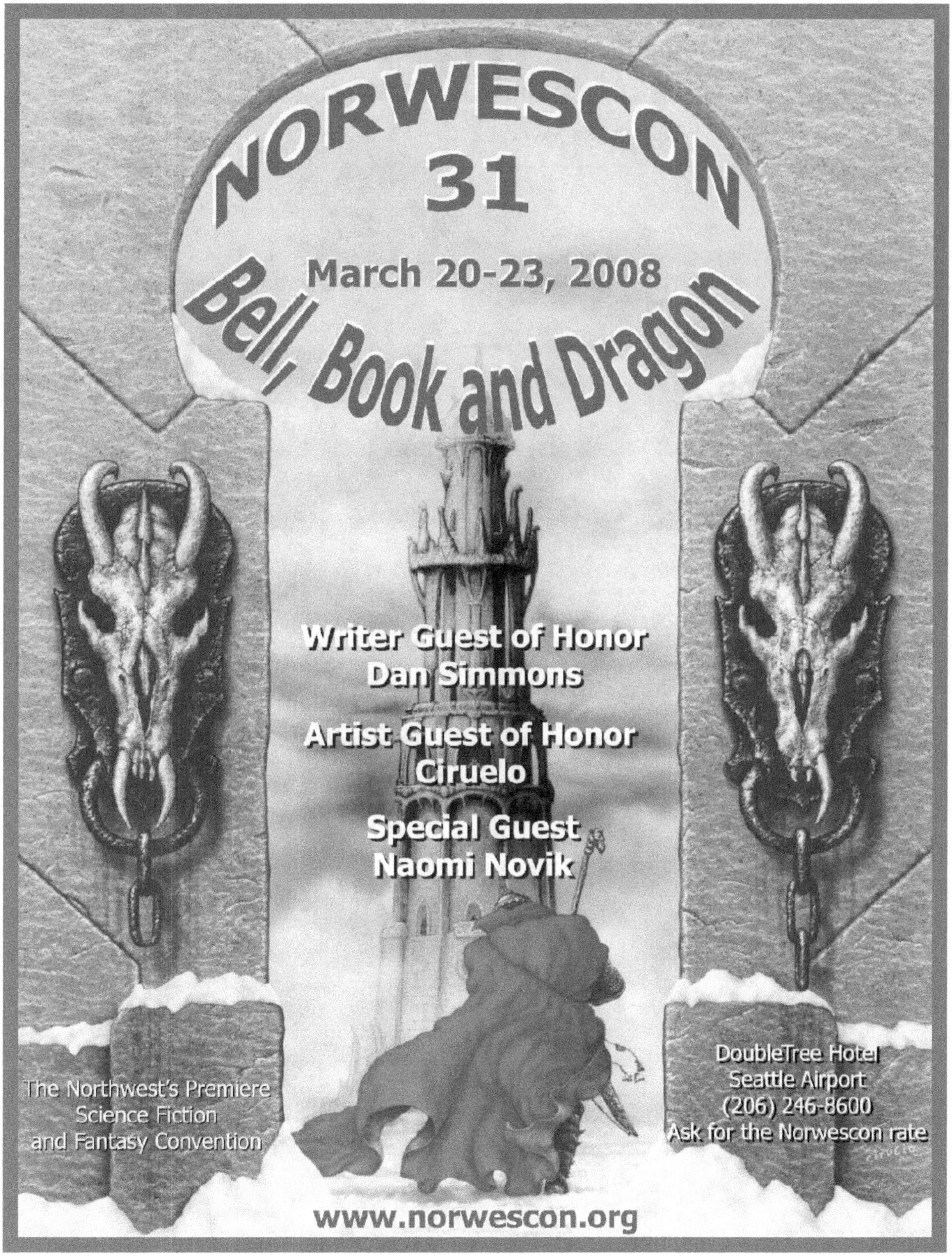

NORWESCON
31
March 20-23, 2008
Bell, Book and Dragon

**Writer Guest of Honor
Dan Simmons**

**Artist Guest of Honor
Ciruelo**

**Special Guest
Naomi Novik**

The Northwest's Premiere
Science Fiction
and Fantasy Convention

DoubleTree Hotel
Seattle Airport
(206) 246-8600
Ask for the Norwescon rate

www.norwescon.org

Lost in Lovecraft

A GUIDED TOUR OF THE DARK MASTER'S WORLD

BY KENNETH HITE

"Remote in the desert of Araby lies the nameless city, crumbling and inarticulate, its low walls nearly hidden by the sands of uncounted ages . . . It was of this place that Abdul Alhazred the mad poet dreamed on the night before he sang his unexplained couplet . . ."
— H.P. Lovecraft,
"The Nameless City"

IT IS NOT Lovecraft who first associates Arabia with horror. Poe famously entitled his masterpiece collection *Tales of the Grotesque and Arabesque* (1840), implying not just fantasy, but a sort of occult, obscurantist, Orientalism that carried with it a specific dark frisson. Where the "grotesques" were satires and gargoyles, the "arabesques" were pure pattern, retraced lines of obsession and madness. Lovecraft was of course a fervent disciple of Poe, but admired Shelley as well – and is there a hint of Shelley's "colossal wreck" from "Ozymandias" (1818) in the "crumbling and inarticulate" ruin of the Nameless City? Even before Shelley, Robert Southey transposed the Gothic to Araby in *Thalaba the Destroyer* (1801) — and William Beckford's lurid Arabian nightmare *The History of the Caliph Vathek* (1786) casts its shadows across them all. Lovecraft read *Vathek* in July of 1921 (six months or so after writing "The Nameless City"), and fell as hard for it as he had for the *Arabian Nights* themselves.

" . . . how many dream-Arabs have the Arabian Nights *bred! I ought to know, since at the age of 5 I was one of them! I had not then encountered Graeco-Roman myth, but found in Lang's Arabian Nights a gateway to glittering vistas of wonder and freedom. It was then that I invented for myself the name of Abdul Alhazred, and made my mother take me to all the Oriental curio shops and fit me up an Arabian corner in my room."*
— H.P. Lovecraft, letter to
Robert E. Howard (1932)

Reading *Vathek* also reinforced Lovecraft's childhood image of Arabia as a fountain of wonders and eldritch knowledge, an image that his later work hints at. In "The Silver Key," we learn that Harley Warren had "prehistoric books and clay tablets smuggled from India and Arabia." Of course, rather than settle for what knowledge merchants and smugglers bring out of Arabia, truly dedicated pilgrims and prophets seek out the source. Moses, Elijah, John the Baptist, Jesus, St. Anthony, St. Benedict — all of them went into the desert to find . . . Something. As does, of course, Lovecraft's own prophet, the "mad Arab" Abdul Alhazred, who (as we learn in "The History of the Necronomicon") "spent ten years alone in the great southern desert of Arabia." And when he returned to the cities, to Damascus, he wrote the *Necronomicon* in answer to Jesus' question in Luke 7:24: "What did you go into the desert to see?"

"That antique Silver Key, he said, would unlock the successive doors that bar our free march down the mightly corridors of space and time to the very Border which no man has crossed since Shaddad with his terrific genius built and concealed in the sands of Arabia Petraea the prodigious domes and uncounted minarets of thousand-pillared Irem. Half-starved dervishes — wrote Carter — and thirst-crazed nomads have returned to tell of that monumental portal, and of the Hand that is sculptured above the keystone of the arch, but no man has passed and returned to say that his footprints on the garnet-strown sands within bear witness. The key, he surmised, was that for which the Cyclopean sculptured Hand vainly grasps."
— H.P. Lovecraft and E. Hoffmann Price,
"Through the Gates of the Silver Key"

Randolph Carter tells us what Alhazred went into the desert to see, and answers the minor conundrum of where he saw it. In "The History of the Necronomicon," Lovecraft tells us that Alhazred "claimed . . . to have found beneath the ruins of a certain nameless desert town the shocking annals and secrets of a race older than mankind." In other words, the Nameless City. But in that earlier tale, the nameless narrator tells us that Alhazred merely "dreamed" of the Nameless City and did not penetrate it. I like to think that our nameless narrator is the bold Northam from Lovecraft's fragment "The Descendant," who "once went into the desert of Araby to seek a Nameless City of faint report, which no man has ever beheld." This meshes well with our narrator's comment, that the Nameless City has been "seen by no living man" until his own misadventure. If true, this would imply that not only Alhazred's journey, but the Yithian-ridden Nathaniel Wingate Peaslee's 1911 attempt (which "roused much attention through a camel trip into the unknown deserts of Arabia") and the similar trip to "the Arabian desert" by the museum-keeper Rogers (of "The Horror in the Museum") all came to nothing.

But Carter gives us the answer. Although the Nameless City holds its own "shocking secrets and annals," the true quest is for "the very Border" of space and time. Hence, Alhazred can approach that Border as Randolph Carter does, by dreaming of it. (Carter, like Alhazred, is also searching for a nameless city in dreams, in a novel with more than a taste of *Vathek*-esque Arabian nightmarishness.) The Nameless City *is* the Border, half-buried in the sand, between life and death, city and desert, anciently on the border between sea and land. It is both and neither, counterpart and reflection. Thus the grotesque Nameless City has a fanciful arabesque twin across the Border, Carter's (and the *Koran*'s) "thousand-pillared Irem." Also called Irâm, Aram, Ubar, Wabar, Omanum Emporium, or Civitas Iboritae, it approaches, paradoxically, namelessness in its own right. Named or nameless, it is likewise a pilgrimage destination for Lovecraftian magi. Not only Alhazred and Carter, but

Alfred Clarendon (in "The Last Test") seemed satisfied with seeking the blasphemies and riches of Irem. Clarendon went not only to the "Hoggar country" (in the Algerian desert) but at least as far as Yemen on the Arabian peninsula as well. There, he met another pilgrim, "an old man who had come back alive from the Crimson Desert — he had seen Irem, the City of Pillars, and had worshipped at the underground shrines of Nug and Yeb. . ." Nug and Yeb, twin deities for twin cities?

> *"Very gorgeous are the descriptions given of Irem, the City of Pillars (as the Koran styles it) supposed to have been erected by Shedad, the latest despot of Ad, in the regions of Hudramaut, and which yet, after the annihilation of its tenants, remains entire, so Arabs say, invisible to ordinary eyes, but occasionally, and at rare intervals, revealed to some heaven-favoured traveller."*
> — from "Arabia," in the *Encyclopedia Britannica* (9th ed.) as copied into H.P. Lovecraft's Commonplace Book

It seems that Lovecraft consciously built the Nameless City as a vaster, deeper, more ancient version – or iteration — of Irem. In the *Arabian Nights,* Irem is a treasure-house city built by the proud King Shaddad determined to create Paradise (in Arabic, *iram*) on Earth. Having spent 70 years in the construction of Irem, Shaddad is killed by Allah before he sets foot in it. The city remains a pristine treasure-house out in the desert sands, with gems lying around for anyone to pick up; a symbolic expression, perhaps, of the eldritch lore available to the diligent seeker. In the *Koran,* Irem is similar to Sodom and Gomorrah — destroyed by Allah for its sinful ways. Pious legend elaborates thusly: The dissolute A'adites of Irem reject the words of Allah's prophet Hud, who invokes Allah's wrath, plaguing Irem with infertility and drought. The A'adite delegation to Mecca gets drunk instead of praying for

deliverance, and that's the last straw for Allah, who destroys Irem in the sight of the returning pilgrims.

Lovecraft builds his own triple parallels to the Koranic legend into the story. Overtly, the Nameless City seemingly spawns the human imitation city Irem: Irem appears as the Nameless City dries out, and the debased remnants of the Nameless City tear "a pioneer of ancient Irem" to pieces before descending into the hollow earth. Historically, the two cities' stories run in tandem: Irem is riding for a fall as Mecca rises, the debased A'adites drive off Hud (the lone "pioneer" from Mecca), and Irem sinks into the sands. What Irem is to Mecca, the Nameless City is to Irem. And symbolically, the various legendary dooms of Irem recur as mirror-image, or black grotesque parody, in "The Nameless City." Irem is destroyed by a Shout from Heaven: the narrator is lured in by "a crash of musical metal" from "some remote depth." Or Irem is destroyed by a powerful wind: the narrator is hurled along by a "shrieking, moaning night wind." Is Irem destroyed by celestial fire, as with Sodom? The Nameless City is forever lit by "some unknown subterranean phosphorescence." Does Irem sink into the sand? The reptile-things dig their own sunken city beneath their temple.

> "Of the cult, he said that he thought the centre lay amid the pathless desert of Arabia, where Irem, the City of Pillars, dreams hidden and untouched. It was not allied to the European witch-cult, and was virtually unknown beyond its members."
> — H.P. Lovecraft, "The Call of Cthulhu"

This parallel between the Nameless City and Irem, the "Atlantis of the Sands," can bear further extension. If the central feature of both is the "city sunken beneath the waste," with strong echoes of prehistory (in the case of Irem) and prehumanity (in the case of the Nameless City), what other sunken city can we look at in this light?

Lovecraft gives us the pointer when he has old Castro locate the center of the Cthulhu cult in (or near) Irem. (Castro's mention of dreams in this context also reinforces our theory about Randolph Carter's Border, as well.) Does the Nameless City "amid the pathless desert of Arabia" seem an odd place for such a thing? Perhaps not so much: "the nightmare corpse-city of R'lyeh" lies on the lifeless floor of the Pacific Ocean, beneath the lone and level waves. A city sunk in a "pathless desert," in other words. The coupling of ocean and desert becomes even more apparent when we remember that the Nameless City was "a mighty seacoast metropolis" slowly engulfed by the sands.

From magical symbolism, we can turn back to literary symbolism. Thus, like "Dagon" and "The Temple" and "The Festival" and "Celephaïs" and the Johansen narrative in "Call of Cthulhu" and *The Dream-Quest of Unknown Kadath* and "Shadow Over Innsmouth," "The Nameless City" is one of the "Oceanic Underworld/Otherworld" motif stories. Again, Lovecraft piles on the parallels. The Nameless City's reptile-things are an aquatic blend of crocodile and seal, the Moore poem quoted mentions the "Sea of Death," and the narrator fights "swirling currents" and a "torrent." Lovecraft repeatedly plays with words like "abyss" and "gulf," which can apply to cav-

Lovecraft builds triple parallels between the Koranic legend of Irem, the Nameless City, and sunken R'lyeh.

erns and ocean deeps alike. The inner world of the reptiles — "a sea of sunlit mist" — resembles both the "Dreamlands" and Y'ha-Nthlei: "glorious cities and ethereal hills and valleys." Finally, Lovecraft took partial inspiration for this tale from a dream he had, in which (in the words of his later commonplace book entry) a man is trapped in a "subterranean chamber — seeks to force door of bronze — overwhelmed by influx of waters." Dreamland, Underworld, Ocean, Otherworld.

> *"For this place could be no ordinary city. It must have formed the primary nucleus and center of some archaic and unbelievable chapter of earth's history whose outward ramifications, recalled only dimly in the most obscure and distorted myths, had vanished utterly amidst the chaos of terrene convulsions long before any human race we know had shambled out of apedom. Here sprawled a Palaeogaean megalopolis . . . ranking with such whispered prehuman blasphemies as Valusia, R'lyeh, Ib in the land of Mnar, and the Nameless City of Arabia Deserta."*
> — H.P. Lovecraft, *At the Mountains of Madness*

In *At the Mountains of Madness*, Dyer compares the Old Ones' city to other "whispered prehuman blasphemies," metaphorically linking "the Nameless City of Arabia Deserta" with Valusia, R'lyeh, and "Ib in the land of Mnar." (Lovecraft's mirroring of Ib and Sarnath within "The Doom That Came to Sarnath" is very similar to his construction of the Nameless City/Irem dyad.) As the Nameless City is covalent with R'lyeh, it is also connected symbolically with Lovecraft's other great cities in the wasteland: the City of the Great Race in the Australian desert and (as Dyer notes) the City of the Old Ones in the "ice desert of the south," to quote Alhazred in "The Dunwich Horror." In all three of those nameless cities, as in R'lyeh, ancient survivors lurk in immense caverns or chambers beneath a lifeless waste. (Despite the contemporary vogue for Mayan ruins, Lovecraft interestingly never treats us to an ancient city covered in a jungle; the closest we get is Sarnath, swallowed by a marshy lake.) And as old Castro tells us, the center of them all is the Nameless City in Arabia, a word that literally means "the waste," deriving as it does from the Hebrew *arav*.

As the cities reflect each other, so do their deserts. The confusion between Kadath in the Cold Waste and "the cold desert plateau" of Leng in "the cold waste north of Inganok" is well known. In "The Hound," Leng is in Central Asia, a manqué perhaps for Tibet. In "The Last Test," Lovecraft makes the Tibet-Arabia connection explicit: the sight of the peculiarly silent and stiff Tibetans (of U-Tsang) "gave Georgina a queer, awed feeling of having stumbled into the pages of *Vathek* or the *Arabian Nights*." The titular hound in the previous story is the "soul-symbol of the corpse-eating cult," reminding us that the lore Lovecraft brought back from Beckford's Arabia was that of the ghouls, who would haunt his fiction thereafter. And the ghouls are, again, emblematic of the waste. In the words (which Lovecraft almost certainly read) of Sir Richard Francis Burton in his notes to the *Arabian Nights*, the ghoul is "an embodiment of the natural fear and horror which a man feels when he faces a really dangerous desert." Lovecraft's (and Beckford's) ghouls haunt the "cities of the dead," the ancient burying grounds of Babylon or Boston. The Nameless City, Pnakotus, Kadath, R'lyeh: All of these cities are graveyards; necropoleis where the corpses don't stay dead. The ghoul, then, is the desert in the midst of the city in the midst of the desert, a recursive ouroborous symbol of Arabia and its nightmares living forever in the midst of death. Nothing, as Shelley says, beside remains. ℮

Next Stop: *Arkham*

The Cryptic

BY DARRELL SCHWEITZER

WITCHCRAFT'S CHARMS

MY HEADLINE COMES from the final section of James Morrow's admirable 2006 novel, *The Last Witchfinder*. I'm not so much reviewing it as beginning this essay by saying that everyone should go out and buy it. It's good. It's entertaining. It's rich and satisfying, not to mention important for what it deals with, and artistically interesting for how the author goes about it.

The Last Witchfinder is the story of Jennet Stearne, the daughter of a witchfinder in late 17th-century England. Witchfinders, you will recall, were professional "cleansers," who rode from town to town, "discovering" witches for a fee. There were several "scientific" tests for discovering Satan's minions in those days. A witch could not recite the Lord's Prayer perfectly. (Anybody with a stutter might therefore be a witch.) She would have a mole or wart, which, if pricked, would not bleed. If you dunked her in a river, she would float, because pure, running water would spit evil out. Jennet's father and later her brother are very good at these techniques, and only at the end of the book does anyone discover (or admit) some of the more "surefire" methods of insuring the witchfinder's income, such as the special pricking knife with a blade that retracts into the handle.

The key to the book, and much of Morrow's impetus for writing it, is that Jennet lives at a crucial time in the development of the human species, right on the cusp where the "Witch Universe" — i.e., the supernatural universe of the Renaissance, in which everything is run and caused by God, angels, and demons — gives way to the clockwork universe of Descartes and the Age of Reason, in which philosophers conclude that the natural world contains its own explanations, and there is no need to turn to an active spiritual will for what we observe. That this view will lead inevitably through Deism to atheism is not something any of the characters in the novel are comfortable with, but it is clearly implied. Much of the message of Morrow's earlier works (*Only Begotten Daughter, Towing Jehovah*) is that humanity will only mature when we outgrow the need for gods and stop inventing them.

But well before that point percolates to the surface, Jennet has many adventures. Her beloved Aunt Isobel is trying to use the newest scientific techniques to "prove" the witch hypothesis. She begins examining tissue from convicted witches' familiars under a microscope, hoping to discover tiny demons in the cells. Alas, this only gets her accused, convicted, and burned at the stake herself. Jennet then devotes her life to overturning the witchcraft laws. It takes her quite a long time, in the course of which she is brought to America, orphaned, captured by Native Americans, rescued, married, has an affair with a young Benjamin Franklin, suffers shipwreck, meets pirates, visits a "utopia" of runaway slaves, authors a series of treatises showing witchcraft to be an impossible crime, and finally puts herself on trial as a test case.

Though it is easy for us with 20/20 hindsight to say that her conclusion should have been "obvious," it would not have been so for a person of her time. All authorities agreed that spirits and witches existed. The New Testament is full of demons — enough so that John Wesley, the founder of Methodism, wrote in his journal in 1768: "The giving up of witchcraft is in effect giving up the Bible." Exactly so; but there is such a thing as knowledge so "dangerous" that no one is ready for it yet, and this must surely be a prime example. Given the premises of the Witch Universe, which are the premises of Bible, the methods of the witchfinders were perfectly logical, and not all the witchfinders were necessarily frauds or lunatics. It would have been the people who said that there was *no* God, that the universe just fell together by happenstance, and that human existence only has such meaning as we ourselves give to it, who would have seemed lunatics, even in the Age of Reason. Not even the Deists went that far. The Age of Existentialism was far in the future, as was the Age of Lovecraft.

If *The Last Witchfinder* were just a historical novel, however admirable, I would not discuss it at such length here; but it's not. First off all, the novel is narrated by a book — specifically, by Newton's *Principia Mathematica*, which informs us at the outset that books are in fact alive, and can author other books, or even, at times, possess human beings to share human experience. (You will be amused, if not entirely surprised, to learn that *Waiting for Godot* is responsible for Windows software documentation.) The result of this conceit is a certain distancing from the straight drama of the story — an effect heightened by slightly old-fashioned dialogue, by no means incomprehensible but not the way we speak today. ("Ah, I see my customer hath finished her tour. I'll warrant she *quite edified*.")

The first level of Morrow's novel is satire, and he produces it wittily. What is more impressive is that, underneath all this, there is a living novel, containing real passion, despair, and horror. The characters grow and change — or, as in the case of Jennet's brother, the titular Last Witchfinder, degenerate. But the distancing effect is necessary, because this is a novel of philosophies and ideas. It's about how our civilization arrived intellectually at the proposition that a non-theistic universe was possible. Morrow is covering nothing less than what could be seen as a major leap in human evolution, which is more important than any set of characters, even the charming Jennet or the odious yet pathetic Dunstan Stearne.

The author has to be in total control of the tone of a book like this. The humor in satire is what makes the ideas stick in the mind; you remember an absurd but meaningful image, something that is funny and also tells us something about ourselves. Who can ever forget Jonathan's Swift's Lilliputian war over which end of the egg you break? But if the author turns shrill and screams at us, we're likely to shut him out. Laughter charms and seduces. It sets us at our ease and makes us receptive to the author's ideas. *The Last Witchfinder* could very easily have been an angry book, or a condescending one. It is not. Morrow has the mix of comedy and drama just right.

Yet what is most intriguing here is something that transcends the novel itself. *Are* we out of the Witch Universe yet? As I write this, I have just read in the newspaper of a case in West Memphis, Ark., where, in 1994, three teenagers were convicted of the murders of three younger boys in a "satanic sacrifice." The initial conviction took place in an atmosphere of hysteria the folks at Salem in 1692 would have understood all too well, led by a latter-day descendant of Dunstan Stearne, a "satanic cult expert" with a mail-order degree. Only thirteen years later has anyone actually ex-amined the evidence and concluded that no DNA of the accused was found, the mutilations of the corpses were done by animals, etc. This is admittedly a more serious case than most 17th-century witchcraft trials, which were merely delusions. Here an actual crime *was* committed by someone. There *were* three corpses. Nevertheless it is very clear that — as we observe all too often in the United States — for all the Jennet Stearnes of the past may have pushed the Witch Universe out the courthouse door, it remains potent and keeps trying to get back in.

Maybe we just don't want to give it up. Every fantasy writer — or reader — has to grapple with this proposition eventually. At the moment her detested but once beloved brother is about to commit spectacular suicide with lightning and a kite in a grim parody of Franklin's famous experiment, Jennet tries to summon up ghosts from her past:

> She shut her eyes and attempted to revive Aunt Isobel's voice, Susan Diggens's specter, all the desires of her mind. Apparently the urge to contact occult entities and do other witchy things lay deep within every person's soul — even those who knew such communion to be impossible. (p.508)

Is that why we write fantasy? Morrow has accomplished an extraordinary feat here, writing a novel about witchcraft and devils without any witchcraft or devils in it. It's so much easier to let the supernatural happen and run with it. The literature of the Witch Universe, such as *The Tragical History of Dr. Faustus* or *Macbeth*, is still much more exciting and dramatic than that of the Age of Reason, for all some people may still read Voltaire's *Candide* or the poetry of Alexander Pope. Reason cannot thrill us with terror. The Romantics knew that, and so, in the latter part of the 18th century, they let the ghosties and ghoulies back in and invented the Gothic novel. Walpole's *The Castle of Otranto* or Lewis's *The Monk* may not have been quite critically respectable, but they were just what the public wanted.

As the form evolved and became the modern supernatural story, the very sort of thing WEIRD TALES publishes, writers learned to avoid the "cheat" ending in which the ghost turns out to be somebody's mad relative running around howling in a sheet. Few Gothics are read anymore, but most of the ones that are, such as *The Monk* or Maturin's *Melmoth the Wanderer*, tend to be those with unrationalized supernatural elements.

Or consider a book like Fritz Leiber's classic *Conjure Wife* (1943). This is a story about a university professor who discovers the faculty wives are witches who perform spells to advance their husbands' careers and thwart those of their rivals. It would be one thing to write a story, possibly a comedy, about a husband combating his wife's silly, superstitious beliefs, but that would not be nearly as dramatic or appealing as what Leiber did write: a horror story in which the protagonist is in mortal danger as soon as he throws away his wife's magical amulets etc., because there *are* such things as demons and now he's defenseless against them.

Think of how many stories you've read in which the basic premise is that the old, folkloristic beliefs are *true*, and the house really is haunted, the dead really do return, there really are zombies or werewolves, or whatever. On one level, the horror story works by confronting its characters with something they "know" to be impossible, and it is this very assault on reason which makes the situation frightening — i.e., the realization that maybe we don't know the rules of how the universe works as well as we think we do. But this does not require that we go back to James Morrow's Witch Universe. H.P. Lovecraft, a skeptic to the core, could not bring himself to believe in a spirit-run universe, so he turned the entire cosmos into a purely materialistic haunted house, inhabited by alien but "natural" spooks, the likes of Cthulhu, Yog-Sothoth, and so on.

Nevertheless, why do we want there to be witches? Admit it, we do. Why is it that *Conjure Wife*, with its very real demons and spells, seems to have much greater emotional power than most stories that lack them? Aside from *The Last Witchfinder,* one of the few other examples I can think of I read more than thirty years ago, Joanna Russ's "The Man Who Couldn't See Devils." It's a story about a young troublemaker or freak or (as his fellows see him) "blind" man, who cannot see devils and monsters when everybody else lives in a world saturated with them. After en-

James Morrow: Master Philosopher

WHY DON'T YOU tell us a little bit about your next book, *The Philosopher's Apprentice?* I am among friends here. I am among people of the science fiction persuasion, so I can say it's a science-fiction novel. But don't tell my publisher that, because they are valiantly portraying me — and this makes real commercial sense — as a man who writers mainstream fiction of interest to people who also like enjoy ideas and epic weirdness. But tonight I'm going to talk about *The Philosopher's Apprentice* as a science-fiction novel and as a cloning story, although I self-consciously avoid the word "cloning" in the text.

The plot centers on a woman scientist who's terminally ill and decides that she needs the ex-

during many persecutions, Russ's protagonist nevertheless concludes that his condition has survival value, and looks forward to the day when people would say, "Those creatures? Oh, they're just legends; they don't exist . . ."

We'd lose a lot of dramatic possibilities if no one could see devils, even on paper. Very possibly fantasy exists precisely because, for all our rational mind has discerned that such things do not exist, our irrational mind requires them. This has profound implications for the very nature of human consciousness. Quite possibly it means that for all James Morrow's fondest wishes, we will never escape the Witch Universe entirely or give up our potentially self-destructive habit (e.g., jihadists plus nukes) of inventing religions and gods. And we have to admit that if we *do* escape it, and the idea of the supernatural is completely dismissed from everyone's mind, the stories will be less good. Very witty perhaps, like the literature of the Age of Reason, but less capable of evoking the deep emotions.

Certainly the fantasy writer does not write to create literal belief in the supernatural. Arguably the supernatural elements in fantasy are symbolic. They clearly are in a work like Ursula Le Guin's *A Wizard of Earthsea*, which gives the phrase "the shadow of his pride" a whole new, literal meaning. Leiber's *Conjure Wife* takes one level of meaning from the perception, perhaps a little whimsical, certainly politically incorrect by today's standards, that men find women mysterious, and that some of their doings are not entirely comprehensible to anyone with a Y-chromosome. But rather than deliver this as a joke, which is what it sounds like, Leiber went for the drama — and the witches.

It's an easy out to say that witches are more fun. The matter is more profound than that. If we really have a Freudian id, if our dreams — and our nightmares — inhabit some specific region (of our brain, of a multi-dimensional universe), then witches know the way there.

Is that why witchfinders were so afraid of them? ☺

His new book, The Philosopher's Apprentice, *is out this March. Morrow offered readers an advance glimpse during a live interview with Darrell Schweitzer at the Free Library of Philadelphia.*

perience of motherhood in toto. Edwina wants to usher an adolescent daughter to the brink of womanhood and beyond. She also wants the joys of having a ten-year-old around the house, the age at which all parents would like to freeze their kids, because they're full of *joie de vivre* and a certain kind of sophistication, but they don't hate you yet. And she also wants a four-year-old. Pre-schoolers are their own reward.

So Edwina creates three genetic copies of herself — and through a lot of biological hand-waving she is able not only to clone herself successfully, but to artificially accelerate the children's maturation to three different ages. So she's got her preschooler and her ten-year-old and her adolescent. These three daughters don't know about each other, because she wants them to focus entirely on her, and in her mind they're all the same child.

Edwina conducts this bizarre experiment on a remote, tropical island, so I get overtones of *The Island of Dr. Moreau* without even trying. She travels around among the three domains in which she has sequestered these kids, and the crazy experiment seems to be working. There's only one problem. The children have no sense of right and wrong. The title of the novel, *The Philosopher's Apprentice*, refers to the fact that Edwina must hire tutors — expert educators and ethicists — to try to implant consciences in these three kids. These are wild children. They have no superegos. Their minds are blank slates.

My main character is the adolescent clone, Londa Sabacthani — a bit of word-play that >>>

>>> some of you may get. In the Gospel According to Saint Matthew, Jesus says, in Aramaic, "Eli, Eli, lama sabachthani," that is, "God, why have you forsaken me?" Londa is the apprentice of the title. The philosopher is a failed Ph.D. candidate, Mason Ambrose, who has gone down in flames during his dissertation defense. Mason undertakes to instruct Londa in morality. He recapitulates the history of western ethics inside her tabula rasa skull — here's what the Stoics had to say about virtue, here's what the Epicureans thought, here's some Aristotle, here's some Kant.

Unfortunately, he also gives her the radical ethics of the Sermon on the Mount, and she goes insane, because, unlike everyone else on the planet, she doesn't understand that you're not supposed to take those ideas seriously.

Besides my nod to *The Island of Dr. Moreau*, there's an homage to Frankenstein going on here. Londa is a monster — not a monster in the sense of a shambling brute played by Boris Karloff. She's a moral monster — she's too good to function in the real world. She has a hypertrophic superego, if you will.

Of course, such an outsize conscience is a recipe for disaster. Londa goes out into the real world, determined to remake our fallen civilization in her own image, and she enacts a lot of crazy schemes. For example, she hijacks a full-scale replica of the *Titanic*. Some plutocrats have rebuilt the ship using the original blueprints, and they're planning to have this great voyage of catharsis. This time the ship won't go down. The capitalists will exorcise the demons of April 14th, 1912. This will pave the way for more entrepreneurial derring-do of the sort that inspired the builders of the original *Titanic*.

But the new ship also runs into an iceberg — a symbolic iceberg. Londa kidnaps all the passengers. In one toss of the net, she catches a whole school of villains, all the capitalists and politicians she holds responsible for the world's ills, so she can rehabilitate them. She forces them to switch places with the third-class passengers, and also the serving staff, and even the stokers. So she gets people who correspond to lobbyists and Bush Administration demagogues shoveling coal down in the boiler room. I had a lot of guilty fun writing that scene.

Isn't this very impulse to reform everybody for their own good what produces most of history's monsters? Indeed. You're absolutely right. Londa has undertaken a program of mandatory virtue, and after a while you actually start to feel sorry for these plutocrats, who are being forced to wait hand-and-foot on the former third-class passengers. The capitalists are treated like dirt. They're not paid enough. They begin to starve. The fumes from the stacks are coming into their cabins because certain environmental regulations have been rescinded. This pollution is in the larger interests of a profitable voyage, so it's completely consonant with the worldview of these aristocrats.

Obviously this is not the answer. Londa's project is doomed, and so is Londa herself. But the novel is not a total downer. Remember, Londa has two sisters. One of them dies violently, but the youngest, by virtue of being the youngest, got to enjoy something resembling a childhood. She is completely sane and sees that there are ways to fight the good fight that are a little less baroque than hijacking a luxury liner.

"Londa is a **monster** ~ not a shambling brute, but a moral monster, too **good** to function in the real world."

I should mention the second major plot thread. In act two, some anti-abortion activists get hold of the same technology that created the sisters. These activists take the tissue from aborted fetuses and accelerate their maturation. This adult version of the might-have-been baby is then sent off to haunt and torment its parents.

I should think these clones would deeply resent having twenty years edited out of their lives, unless they're compensated by greater longevity later on. If you're raised from embryo to the physical equivalent of twenty in one year, you've just lost a quarter of your life. Exactly. That's one of the themes of the novel. You've got to have a childhood. You have to go through all sorts of experiences. These walking fetuses, these immaculoids, as they're called by the anti-abortion forces, are clearly just pawns. Their only purpose is to make possible the most spectacular anti-abortion protest ever staged.

So when is the book coming out? March of 2008.

Anything beyond that? My editor was pleased with the reception of *The Last Witchfinder*. It was not a box-office hit, but it sold respectably. So I pitched her some new ideas. She didn't like them. She said, "Those are too weird," which I think was her way of saying, "They're science fiction ideas, Jim. Come on."

So when I went home from that lunch, I was a little down, and my dear wife Kathy said, "Jim, there's a squid on the mantelpiece you're not noticing. You've been obsessed with Charles Darwin ever since I've known you, and your editor wants you to write a historical novel. Why don't you put two and two together?"

I said, "But nothing ever happened to Charles Darwin. That's why he's never been at the center of a novel." Wait, I tell a lie. There is a dopey novel by Irving Stone called *The Origin*, which is nothing more than a dull Darwin biography with made-up dialogue inserted into it. But anyway, I said to Kathy, "Once he went around the world and came back with the bad news about God, he dissected barnacles for ten years. That doesn't sound like drama to me."

But I thought about the problem some more, and finally I came up with a storyline. I imagined a society of Victorian freethinkers who float an enormous cash prize. They want to settle this damn God question. They believe there's been enough theological, philosophical, and scientific work done on the problem that someone can step forward with a proof. So my Percy Bysshe Shelley Society offers a ten-thousand-pound purse to anybody who can convince the jury, which includes a careful balance of skeptics and believers, one way or the other. And so my heroine, Chlöe, a mighty spunky woman — once again I'm writing a feminist novel — says, "I don't really care whether God exists or not, but I want the

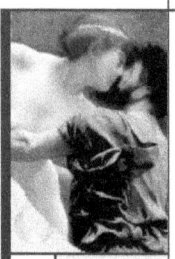

money. In fact I need the money. My father is in a workhouse. He's going to die."

She already happens to have a job taking care of the animals Darwin brought back from the Galapagos. I'm bending history a bit here. I have Darwin returning with giant tortoises and huge marine iguanas. My heroine is in charge of this private zoo. She overhears Darwin saying, "I could easily collect the Percy Bysshe Shelley Prize, but of course I won't. I'm a serious scientist. Going after the gold would sully my reputation forever." So Chlöe breaks into Darwin's study and starts copying his notes.

Darwin was a very kindly soul. He makes the worst possible villain for those Fundamentalists who insist on demonizing him. Yes, he was an agnostic. Yes, he walked away from the Church of England. Yes, he rejected his wife's Unitarian beliefs, which were not the Unitarian beliefs of today: Unitarianism back then was pretty conventional and salvationistic. Darwin, who is a decent man by almost any definition of the word — decent at a level that puts the whole Jerry Falwell crowd to shame — nevertheless he becomes furious and throws Chlöe out of the house. He tells her, "Never darken my door again. I can't trust you. No, you cannot present my specimens to the jury in an attempt to claim this prize."

So Chlöe decides that she has no other choice — and believe me, it's more plausible than it sounds – but to go around the world herself and collect these animals. So she does. She has many Jennet Stearne-like adventures.

The message of the Darwin novel will be ambiguous. I think ambiguity is the *sine qua non* of almost all worthy fiction. That's why I tried to give the witchfinders their due, and why I tried to understand the strategists in *This Is the Way the World Ends*. The pro-choice/anti-abortion discourse in *The Philosopher's Apprentice* is pretty unsettling, no matter where you stand on the issue. I think that's why God made fiction — to get readers having thoughts they've never had before, not to get them confessing their sins or agreeing with the author's philosophical or political opinions.

If you tune in the war that Americans keep fighting over Charles Darwin — Europeans, by the way, are appalled by this brouhaha — you often hear a simple, soothing, comforting argument from people who should know better. It goes like this. "There is no incompatibility between evolution and theism. Darwin simply described the biological laws that God laid down, laws that have played out over time in ever shifting physical environments. Nature obviously has a divine component and a material component — what's the big deal?"

Well, there are enormous problems with that answer. Extinction, for example. On first principles, extinction would not seem to be the modus operandi of a benevolent creator. The proponents of "natural theology" are simply not confronting the unimaginable quantities of pointless death that, if Darwin got it right — and I'm persuaded he did — have caused the biosphere to look and behave the way it does.

What is the title of this book? The working title is *Galapagos Regained*, an allusion to *Paradise Regained*. I don't know if that title will prosper. I wanted to call this book — *The Philosopher's Apprentice* — I wanted to call it *Prometheus Wept*, an allusion to the shortest verse in the Bible. Everybody in the novel is involved in some sort of Promethean activity, which, depending on your point of view, is either arrogant or noble.

But both the U.K. editor and the U.S. editor said, "No, *Prometheus Wept* is too high-falutin'. It assumes that the reader is some kind of intellectual." So I suspect *Galapagos Regained* won't make the cut either. Let me hasten to add that I have wonderful editors, and that the new title, *The Philosopher's Apprentice*, has won me over. It's both a thoughtful and a commercial title, so I can't complain. ℰ

Lament for a One-Legged Lady

BY LISA M. BRADLEY

A mortician's daughter,
she always assumed
the empty cello case
in the secondhand store window
was a voluptuous coffin
propped open to release
the velvet-kissed ghost
of a one-legged lady.
She'd inch into the display
and rifle through the loose pages
of that lady's last will and testament,
tilt her head to listen
to the stale whispers
of sheet music.
As she pondered this foreign script,
the meaning of bereft and
blackened circles
trapped within lines,
she wondered where the corpse went,
half hoped it had escaped,
like these winged spheres
breaking free
of five brittle bars.

The February 1932 issue must have evoked cries of delight at the time. Despite the subsequent fame of H.P. Lovecraft, Robert E. Howard, and Clark Ashton Smith, it was Seabury Quinn who was actually the most popular contributor *during* the magazine's golden age. The cover by artist C.C. Senf, showing a naked woman about to be nailed to a cross by red-hooded fiends, illustrates the first and only serial featuring Quinn's French psychic detective Jules de Grandin, who would herein be battling the supernatural steadily through six installments of "The Devil's Bride."

On a somewhat loftier level, the issue includes "Night and Silence" by Maurice Level, a mysterious French writer (who may have been a woman) specializing in *conte cruels*. The Gallic strain continues with the concluding installment of "The Haunted Chair" by Gaston Leroux, the author of *The Phantom of the Opera*, and a serialized reprint of *The Wolf Leader* by Alexandre Dumas, author of *The Three Musketeers*.

Other WEIRD TALES regulars are also well in evidence this issue — notably Robert E. Howard with a Cthulhu Mythos tale, "The Thing on the Roof," and science-fiction writer Edmond Hamilton with one of his few horror stories, "The Three from the Tomb." — *D.S.*

OUR BIG ANNIVERSARY SPECIAL! Join us as we celebrate 85 years of WEIRD TALES. For starters, it's the only place you'll find out who made our list of **The 85 Weirdest Storytellers of the Past 85 Years!** Then there's dark-fantasy superstar **China Miéville**, holding forth on good monsters, bad movies, and fiction's hidden ideologies. We finally see the *Weird Tales* debut of novelist **Sarah Monette**, who brings us the latest supernatural exploit of jittery museum archivist Kyle Murchison Booth. And — what was that other thing? Oh, yes: an all-new **Elric of Melniboné** novella by the one and only **Michael Moorcock!**

PLUS: Cherie Priest talks steampunk art; original fiction by Tanith Lee, Rachel Swirsky, Ramsey Shehadeh, and John Kirk; a serious look at the science of resurrection, *Dune*-style; and more!